HAUNTED BY THE DEVIL

THE DEVIL'S SOCIETY
BOOK ONE

KINSLEY KINCAID

Note from the Author

Please be aware this book contains many **dark themes** and subjects that may be uncomfortable/unsuitable for some readers. This book contains **heavy themes** throughout. Please keep this in mind when entering Haunted by the Devil. Content warnings are listed on authors' social pages & website.

This book and its contents are entirely a work of fiction. Any resemblance or similarities to names, characters, organizations, places, events, incidents, or real people are entirely coincidental or used fictitiously.

If you find any genuine errors, please reach out to the author directly to correct it. Thank you.

This book is intended for 18+ only.

PLAYLIST

The Devil in I - Slipknot
I Put A Spell On You - Annie Lennox
The Grim Weeper - Diggy Graves
Closer - Nine Inch Nails
Look What You Made Me Do - Taylor Swift
Change(In the House of Flies) - Deftones
I Write Sins Not Tragedies - Panic! At The Disco
DAYWALKER(feat. CORPSE) - mgk, CORPSE
Straightjackets & Roses - Diggy Graves
I like the way you kiss me - Artemas
Helena - My Chemical Romance
King Of My Heart - Taylor Swift
TEETH(feat. Diggy Graves) - WesGhost
Dead! - My Chemical Romance
Antarctica - $uicideboy$
Dancer in the Dark - Chase Atlantic

Dethrone - Bad Omens
Hello Sunshine - Palaye Royale
On Some High - SEBASTIAN PAUL
Kool-Aid - Bring Me The Horizon
Would've, Could've, Should've - Taylor Swift

Spotify Playlist

Elijah Sinclair is a Psychopath

*When you are contemplating body bags with or without
handles. To dig a shallow or deep grave. Know it's because
we all have a little piece of him inside of us.
So spread your wings, little bats. Embrace all the sides of
yourself. Because it is a fucking blast.*

"He's been watching you all night." Butch rumbles in front of me as I pour him another whiskey.

Shrugging my shoulders, "It's fucking creepy, but he hasn't done anything and keeps ordering drinks. He's harmless. Most likely lacks social etiquette."

Butch tilts his head, not buying what I am selling.

"Just be extra cautious when you leave tonight. You never know. It's the quiet, weird ones you need to watch out for. Creepy fucks."

I laugh. Not because it's funny. Because he's right. Anytime you hear of some crazy shit going down on the news, it's always the quiet ones.

"I promise Butch. Plus, I always have pepper spray nearby," I reassure him, patting my pants pocket. It seems to appease the old guy. Butch means well. He is a regular at the bar, I have been serving him six nights a week for the past six months. My mom knows the owner, I am not technically old enough to serve until tomorrow, my twenty-first birthday, but he said 'if I don't tell, he wouldn't either', so here we are, the best unkept secret around. This town is small enough that everyone knows how old I am, but nobody actually gives a fuck.

"You know…" My co-worker Amy starts talking next to me, "I've heard things… You see that tattoo on his arm. Of the bat wings, like they are actually coming out of his skin…" Looking over at her, she bites her lip like she is too nervous to continue.

"Go on, Amy. Tell me your theory," I encourage, even though I'm completely over this. Butch has been on about the guy for the last fifteen minutes. Amy has been wide eyeing me each chance she gets.

"It's the tattoo they get once they join The Chapel." She finally spits it out in a hushed tone. Her eyes are trying to project the same, this boy means danger.

Amy has been serving him all night and hating each moment of it.

Turning my nose up, I scrunch my face dismissing her theory. "You think he is a member of The Chapel? The freaky devil cult? They are rumored to be located miles away from here, in Blackwood. Why would one come all the way to Crest for a drink? It doesn't make sense."

Amy frantically covers my mouth, her eyes wide. "Not so loud. He will hear you!" Sticking my tongue out, I lick her palm and she flinches away.

"They are dangerous, Rain!" Amy hisses at me. She's so insanely serious, I almost feel bad messing with her.

Everyone within a ten-mile radius of Blackwood knows the rumors of The Chapel. In my opinion, they exist but not to the degree that the stories build them up to. Rituals involving blood sacrifices, fires with chanting, and having an underground laier where they hold their secret meetings seem a tad too out there to be true. I definitely believe they do some crazy shit, like calling upon the Devil and thinking they have powers or whatever, but the rest is bullshit.

Smirking, I decide to mess with her a little bit more.

"He's kind of hot, though. You have to admit it. Should I take him home? Ring my birthday in with a bang? I bet he is into some crazy shit."

He's been sitting in a booth all night. Back to the wall, his long legs propped on the seat. His hair is black and shaggy, falling over his forehead. Wearing a black tee, he's covered in ink all the way to his black painted fingertips. Black distressed skinny jeans and loosely laced black combat boots finish the look. His face has remained expressionless the entire time. His full lips remain neutral, with the exception of when he uses his teeth to play with his lip ring. A septum piercing glints in the dim overhead light whenever he tilts his head to take a sip of his drink. It's hard to tell from here what color his eyes are, but they seem dark. He doesn't look much older than me.

And I know the exact tattoo Amy is referencing on his arm. I may have been looking back at him from time to time. My eyes linger longer than they should have been. There is no doubt he has noticed.

I find him curious, not scary.

My energy is drawn to him, I can't explain it, but there is a pull. His staring all night hasn't made me feel uncomfortable once. It is actually oddly comforting. I don't believe we have met before, his face is memorable, and I do not remember it.

Breaking me out of my thoughts, Amy grabs my exposed arm, pulling me into the tiny kitchen located on the other side of the bar wall. "This isn't funny! People talk because bad things happen when they come around. Sure, maybe some of it isn't true. But the rumors have to have some truth to them."

I can tell I'm stressing her out. Which was fun, until it wasn't. Amy is one of the sweetest people I know.

"I'll be ok. He's harmless. I have pepper spray in case he follows me to my car or bathroom. I always have it with me on late shifts. Amy, I promise. It's ok." She lets go of me and wraps me in a big hug, "Thank you." She whispers while nodding against my shoulder.

Letting go, I step back and look at her, "I'm going to finish topping up my guys at the bar, then cash out. It's going to be ok. If he wanted something from me, he wouldn't have wasted his money and time here all night. He would have gotten what he came for and left." Reassuring her.

Walking back out of the backroom, I look for him. Except the booth is empty. My head tilts, confused. A few bills are under his empty glass.

He left. Just like that.

This doesn't make sense.

Not that any of it has, but this definitely doesn't.

Amy comes up behind me and pauses next to me.

"See. I told you," telling her as if I am not phased. My eyes shift around the room. I can still feel him.

Where is he?

CHAPTER 2

RAIN

"Happy birthday, my sweet girl." The smell of mom's perfume fills my nose. Lavender and pear notes can be detected.

I'm in bed, home late from my shift. It's well past one in the morning, meaning it is indeed my birthday. Mom stays up waiting regardless. Making sure I get home safe. It's sweet, I tell her she doesn't need to, but she does each and every single time.

"Thanks mom, night."

She turns off my bedroom light and closes my door. The old floorboards creek beneath her with each step, until I hear her own bedroom door close.

Yesterday was my last day being twenty. Today, which is only a couple hours old, I turned twenty-one, officially of drinking age. Not that it matters, no one actually ever waits until then to have alcohol. I work in a bar, for fuck's sake.

This is also the last check mark needed for the 'what makes you an adult' checklist in the eyes of the state of North Carolina.

I still live with my mom in my childhood home, still sleeping in my childhood room.

I am the product of a one-night stand. I've never met or known my father. My mom has never brought him up, unless I have. Which was only when I was old enough to realize I was one of the kids in class who only had one parent instead of two.

It's never bothered me, just having my mom. It's always felt right being just the two of us. I didn't need him. I didn't know what it was like to have him. So there is no void or resentment.

I am one of the few left here from my high school graduating class, most left for college the first chance they got. Not me, I have no idea what I want to do with my life. Mom doesn't pressure me. She says I have my whole life to figure it out, which I love, but at the same time I feel stuck. What is my purpose? Sometimes it does frustrate me, but most times I just go with the flow and hope one day it clicks.

They do say it happens when you least expect it.

My eyes are heavy. My body is sore after working a ten-hour shift. One server didn't show up for an earlier shift, so I went in early. I didn't see that guy after my shift either. The feeling of him being around never left me. And still hasn't. It's such a strange feeling. One that I am not sure I can describe.

Thankfully, I'm off today.

Happy birthday to me is the last thought to cross my mind as I drift asleep.

My eyes open rapidly.

My heart is racing. I'm too nervous to move. There is someone in my room. The curtain which normally blocks my window is missing. The bright moon shines through the now open window. A slight breeze can be felt from where I lay in bed.

Someone is in my room.

They have to know I am awake. The reflection of the moon's light must be reflecting off my face, my eyes glistening in it. They have to know.

My senses feel heightened. What I cannot see, I must be able to hear.

Before I feel brave enough to move my body, a deep voice startles me. They are next to me.

"Don't do it."

My eyes squeeze shut. Panic.

Tears slowly trickle down my cheeks as I try to contain any emotion.

I'm going to die. My mom is going to find me, dead, in my bed when she wakes up. She is going to need years of therapy to get the image of my dead body out of her head. Possibly even move away from our home, my childhood home, to escape the memory of my twenty-first birthday. I wonder how he will do it. Slow and painfully, or quick and easy. I hope it's quick and easy. This way, people won't have to lie to my mother when they say, '*It probably happened so fast, she didn't suffer,*' compared to if it is slow and painful.

Unless, has he already killed my mother?

Saving me for last. But that wouldn't make sense. My window is the one open. He hasn't left my room.

A shadow crosses over me as a cloth is pressed against my mouth and nose.

Before I can fight it, I breathe it in. The smell is strong as my eyes become heavy again.

Just as I pass out, a wave of realization washes over me.

It's him.

CHAPTER 3
RAIN

Water droplets echo. A chill has turned into shivers. My teeth chatter against one another, and my feet feel like ice. Earthy scents invade my nose. Like I am outside, it's damp and fresh but also tainted with what could be sulfur, possibly. With heavy eyes, I rub my hand on the hard surface beneath me. Sand, small pebbles, crushed rock and dirt. It feels dry against my hand. My head is pounding like I have just been hit with a ton of bricks. With every ounce of energy I have left, I begin to open my eyes. It's dark, and shadows of orange light flicker along the wall in front of me.

A sneeze escapes me, which elevates the pounding in my head further. My face scrunches in distress. Slowly sitting up, I lift my head off the ground. It feels heavy as my neck is strained and stiffened by it. My hands go to my temples and begin rubbing them slowly to help alleviate the pain.

As my eyes become fully open, I try to focus on what's around me. Confusion takes over. Where am I? The wall in front of me is not a wall at all, but a dark stone. The light fluttering against it is fire. A single torch is lit, attached to the wall by what seems to be a metal holder. It's completely silent all around, as a crackle from it startles me. Holding my breath, I wait for another, but it doesn't come. My eyes are mesmerized by the beautiful color and dance of it. Shaking my focus away, I continue to move my body, still unsure about where I am and why.

My knees bend as my bare feet begin to rotate my body, and my bottom stays in place as I move. Loose rock and dirt lining the ground stick to my feet and rub against the exposed skin that my sleep shorts aren't covering. The stone wall feels like it is never-ending, forever wrapping around me in this small and damp space, that is until an opening appears. The opening is blocked by steel bars, similar to what I imagine a jail cell would be like. They are attached to flat pieces lining the top and bottom, which seem to allow the door to slide open. A steel padlock is on one end, closed shut.

My heart sinks as my body begins to move on its own. I'm on my hands and knees, crawling toward the bars. Curiosity has taken over, or it has only trumped my fear at this moment.

The space is small, maybe six foot by six foot but I'm not sure. Math and measurements aren't my thing. It only takes me a few movements to reach the cell door. My hand reaches through the tight opening, and my fingers touch the lock. It's cold against me as I slowly try to pull it down to not make a noise, but it doesn't budge.

Letting it go softly, so not to rattle it against the bars, my brain begins to catch up with my body. Panic takes over my curiosity.

Looking up, another torch is on the stone wall across from me, lighting the area. My eyes shift from one side to another, trying to see where the long hall goes. There is no one else around.

I am alone.

As realization washes over me, biting my lip, I scurry backwards until I feel the cold stone behind me, ridged against my back. My head falls back on it as my eyes close, and my breathing becomes more rapid with each breath. The last thing I remember is being in bed. It was my birthday, and my mom had just said good-night to me. Then I felt him, he was close. His presence was unmistakable— the same strange but comforting feeling I had when he was at the bar most of the evening, watching me. Then, out of nowhere a cloth covered my face, it had a strong smell and everything went black.

Someone took me. Someone has taken me. No one is going to find me here.

Tears stream down my face as I think about my mom going into my room and finding an empty bed. As she frantically looks for me, she will see all my things still there, along with my car and phone. Her only child disappears on her twenty-first birthday. This is going to break her. Absolutely ruin her.

I hope that when they or whoever they are, kill me. They'll leave my body somewhere my mother will find me. Or someone else nearby. To give her closure and peace instead of forever wondering, *is she still alive?* Forever living in hope and what if's.

I don't want her to live a life like that. I need her to have closure.

My brain immediately goes to death because statistics say this will only end one way, with me dead. People very rarely come out of a kidnapping alive. It's too risky for whomever takes them; the captured would tell the police everything they remember, resulting in the kidnappers being arrested. So what's the point?

Then another wave of realization consumes me.

As the thought enters my mind, my lip quivers in fear.

I bring my knees close to my chest and wrap my

arms around my legs in an effort to protect myself before anything has even happened.

But first, they will assault me.

The police or medical examiner will have to tell her that. Disclose it all. If I thought her finding my dead body would ruin her, this would end her. She would picture it and think of it every time she closed her eyes or when sitting alone outside in the morning having her coffee.

I want to hide and shrink away so they can't find me or forget I am even here.

I'm so scared.

CHAPTER 4

RAIN

I fell asleep. I haven't a clue how long I stayed sitting against the wall before my eyes finally fluttered shut. Exhausted and overwhelmed, it came easily. I'm not sure how long I was out for or how long I have been up now. My mouth is dry, and a slight headache still lingers. I would do anything for some water right now.

The fire is still lit, and it dances against the stone. Watching it has helped pass the time.

I don't feel him.

I've tried to force it. Search for his energy to meet mine. But there's nothing. He isn't here. Why would he let them take me? Was it him? It couldn't be. Nothing about the last twenty-four hours has made sense; it could be longer than that by now, I can't be sure.

One thing I am sure about is that I fucking felt him just before my world went black.

No one has come to check on me since. It's been eerily quiet. The water droplets and the fire are the only things I have heard. Being left alone to my own thoughts is torture; it wanders every time to my ending, to the what-ifs and maybes. There's no point in giving myself false hope. I am typically an optimistic person, but in this situation, it's hard to be.

The near silence of the space is deafening. My mind is starting to play tricks on me. The fear of the unknown is amplifying it. With each drip of water that echoes through the cave, my mind goes *tick tock, tick tock*. The few times that the drips stopped, I scurried making sure my back was against the wall, with my eyes closed pretending to be asleep. My mind convinced me someone was coming. I'm not sure how long I stayed like that each time, but long enough to realize I was no longer thinking rationally.

My eyes have been watching for shadows against the rock wall outside of my cell. I have spent hours fixating on it. Whenever the flame flickers, my heart pounds thinking it's been disturbed by a person. Then I wait like I did with the drops, holding my breath for someone to pop out, but they never come. If they are capable of taking me, they are capable of things I can't even envision.

The sound of a male clearing his throat catches my

attention. My eyes look in the direction that it's coming from. I didn't even hear anyone coming, how long have I been in my head? How long has he been watching me? This is a stranger, but not my stranger. I don't feel *him*.

This person before me, on the other side of the bars, is in a dark black robe. From his feet to the hood on the top of his head, it covers his entire body, with long sleeves that hang over his hands.

A white mask with an intricate gold-painted design around both eyes and over the bridge of the mask's nose. It has an opening for his eyes, two for the nostrils, and a small hole for the mouth. My heart sinks, taking him in. My eyes watch as his hand moves to his pocket, getting what he reached in for, he moves it out toward the lock. Gripping the lock with his other hand, he places a dark key into it. As he twists, the lock pops open and he pulls it off the door without saying a word. It's hard to tell if he is looking at me or at the cell door. It's too dark to see his eyes, with the mask holes casting shadows over the small openings.

He begins to slide the door open; it's loud against the hard stone ground, scraping it as it goes. I hate this sound, but I don't flinch as I don't want him to see how it affects me. As it reaches the end of the opening, he stops and moves to stand in the opening, dropping the lock at his feet with the key still inside. Is he testing me?

Neither of us do anything. I never take my eyes off him, waiting for him to make the next move. I assume it's a male, but it could very well be a female with a deep voice. Either way, I know I am fucked.

They step forward, and black shoes peek under the long black fabric. The loose gravel crunches beneath with each step taken. It only takes them a couple steps for them to be standing directly over me. Their head tilts down toward me slightly as my eyes move up. Then, they reach out their hand, their bare skin is exposed. I don't move. My body trembles; it's been through a lot and has done a great job trying to protect me, but I'm not sure it will cope with what is bound to come next. I'm still sitting still, not moving as they tilt their head toward their hand, coaxing me to take it. Swallowing the little saliva I have, I take a deep breath and raise my trembling hand to theirs as I begin to rise.

I haven't stood up since I woke up here the first time. My legs are stiff and filthy, I am still only in my sleep shorts and tee. Their hands are rough and big, confirming this is definitely a male. As I fully stand, my head is maybe two feet from the top of this prison, this person's head is inches away from touching it. He drops his hand from mine, turns around, and begins to walk toward the open cell door. He must expect I will follow.

And I do.

Tiny sharp pieces of broken rock embed themselves into the bottom of my feet as I walk; some cut against my flesh, but that is the least of my worries. Because this man is leading me to my death. I am certain. My body is trembling, my teeth chatter and I want to cry, but my eyes are so dry that nothing comes out.

Leading us down a long hallway, it is also lit by the same torches as my cell. My fingertips brush against the cold, dark stone that surrounds us. We are underground somewhere, but for the life of me I can't figure out where. As I continue to take in my surroundings, I notice the area becomes more lit up, more torches line each side of us, along with a low humming noise which can be heard. My brows furrow, trying to concentrate. Is it just a hum, or are they saying something? Not paying attention, I don't realize the man in front of me has stopped walking, and I walk into his back. Caught off guard, I stumble backwards and almost apologize out of habit, but I cover my mouth with my hands and stop myself. He is unphased by it, not even turning around. Looking around to see why we have stopped, I see we are standing within a stone archway. He steps further inside the space while still blocking my view. As he turns his body to the side, it exposes a larger room within the cave area, which is lined with over a dozen people, at least.

All of them are wearing the same long black cloaks,

hoods over their heads, and white masks with the gold design.

My eyes move around in the room while my brain tries to figure out if I can place any of these people or this place. None of this is ringing a bell for me.

I wish I could feel him. Unease and terror ripples over me. Nervously, I start picking at my nails as all the white masks look at me in silence.

Then, a loud voice echoes in the space, shocking me as my head turns towards it.

"Rain, my girl. Welcome home."

CHAPTER 5

RAIN

The man standing at the front of the room, who welcomed me home, knows my fucking name. He stands taller than the rest, wearing the same white mask as everyone else. Others stand before him, there aren't a lot of them, maybe twenty or so. But it makes the small space feel full. His black cloak also has gold trim decorating it. On the breast there is a design that I can't quite make out from where I am standing. My fingers rake through my disheveled and long black hair, which is in desperate need of a brush.

Where the fuck am I?

Along with the torches lining the area, white candles decorate the perimeter of the area. The wax is melting onto the dirt floor. I swallow, opening my mouth to speak, to demand some sort of answer but no words escape me. I am completely frozen.

"Ah, my child. No need to say anything at all. You are here to observe this evening. We have a special night planned for our followers, for you," The deep, captivatingly calm voice explains.

The man who escorted me here grabs my arm, his grip is tight as he begins leading me towards the front. I try to pull away, but he grips me harder. "Don't bother fighting. It is of no use."

The same loud voice speaks to me again. I nod my head once, in defeat. He isn't wrong.

As we approach, the followers begin stepping aside to clear a path. My eyes examine each one, all in the same robes and masks. The man standing at the front seems to be special, only his robe has the gold trim and emblem. There is a row of men whose backs continue to face me, they do not move like the others did. My handler and I stop, finally building up the courage, I go to speak but he stops me.

He nods his head to the people in the front, and they all move to the side. My heart drops into my stomach when my eyes land on who is lying there, and my knees shake as my lip trembles. My handler lets go of me as I fall to the ground.

All color has to have left my body as shock sets in.

Covering my mouth, I shake my head in absolute disbelief, "No. No, this can't be."

"Oh, but it is." His voice echoes, it sounds further away than it did just moments ago. My eyes are focused on the sight before me, everything has disappeared around me as my body still trembles. Tears race down my cheeks, and suddenly I feel so cold that my teeth chatter.

"Rain, look at me." His authoritative tone causes my head to look up at him. His head slants as he looks at me. Why does he know my name?

The emblem is clear now, on his robe. The outline of bat wings is etched into it. Each peak of the wing has a line running down to the bottom. The way it is done makes it appear as though they are flying out of the fabric.

I recognize that symbol.

"Society dictates, no harm to women and children. Save them first. Protect them. But why? We do not see gender. We see good and evil. Our God shows them to us, and we honor his request. We do not follow society's norms. Tonight is a very special night, my sweet Rain. You have come home to me, to us. We must celebrate your arrival, your future." He interrupts my thoughts. Speaking as he steps down from where he is standing. He is now on even ground with me and the others. Gravel crunches beneath his shoes with each step towards the long, dark wood table before us. Reaching out, his finger brushes against it as he passes, then reaches me.

"Don't be scared. She was shown to us before your birthday. It's okay." He reassures me while standing over me.

"You are fucking vile. Get away from me!" I screech back. I am sobbing, and inconsolable. Nothing about this is okay. He is delusional. He is a fucking monster.

My nostrils flare in rage as my lungs scream into the room. No one reacts, no one except for the man standing in front of me taunting me and laughing at me.

Then, I feel *him*. In my body, bones and soul, his energy. He is here. My eyes frantically look around, but nothing.

"My boy. Wake up the evil that lingers in our presence. I can smell her rot from here. It is eating her from the inside. All is too late, she cannot be saved." He declares.

Loud slaps can be heard echoing in the room. At one point I think her skin must have cracked open from the sounds of the hand smacking her, over and over again.

Catching me off guard, my handler grabs me by the crook of my arm, thrusting me off the dirty ground and onto my feet. His hand tightly wraps around me, squeezing until it hurts. But I don't wince, refusing to show him I am in pain.

My brain is racing with only one thing: I need to get to her. I need to save my mom.

Mustering up all the strength I can, I shout, "My mom is not an evil person."

The man in front of me, the leader of this fucked-up place steps aside. My mom, who is naked, is being held down by four people. Her cheek facing me is bright red.

"Let her go!" I cry.

Another stands at her head, his arms are crossed over his chest. I assume he is the one who was possibly slapping her. He is the only one not wearing a mask, but instead his face is painted similar to a skull.

My mom's face turns towards me as she mouths, '*I love you, my girl*'. A single tear rolls down her face. My chest heaves, still uncontrollable sobbing, and wishing I would just wake up. This is all a dream, please wake the fuck up. I will do anything for this to all be a dream.

My silent pleas are interrupted, "Do it my boy, show us how you earned your wings." The man instructs.

As I look at the man again who is standing at her head, I feel *him*. Why isn't *he* stopping this or helping me? *He* has to be feeling this too. Where is *he*?

His eyes pierce into mine, they almost seem familiar. He doesn't take them off me as he uncrosses his arms.

A silver blade is revealed in his hand. Without taking his eyes off of me, he lifts his arm over my mother, directly above her throat. My breathing stops, and my eyes widen as I start to understand what is coming next. Shaking my head, faint *'no's'* sneak out between my lips.

Everything seems like it is moving in slow motion now. His hand moves down, plunging the sharp tip into the thin skin on her neck. He doesn't stop there; while his eyes remain on me, his tattoo-covered hand grips the handle harder, twisting it ninety degrees.

My mom coughs at the movement, and blood begins pouring out of her mouth. She tries to get out of the strong hold, her arms and legs fidget but they do not budge. With each cough, more blood gushes from her.

Turning her head to face me, her eyes are hooded as tears of blood fall down her cheek. Then, the crimson red begins to drip out of her nose.

"Mommy…" I don't know if I said this out loud or just in my head. I feel like I am no longer in my own body as I watch this.

The man holding the blade never lets go of it.

Looking up at him, I mouth to him *please*, trying to plead with him to help her. His eyes remain on me, and his body doesn't move.

Fucking bastard.

He is completely unaffected by the horrific scene he has caused.

Defeat starts to settle in as I watch her die. No one is going to help her.

The only parent I have ever had, the one person who truly loves me, is leaving me too soon.

"Mommy, no, please don't go. Please stay with me. Mommy."

Her head gets heavy as it falls against the table. Looking into my eyes, she blinks at me once more before life fades from them. She is gone.

"I fucking hate you. You bastard, I hate you." I manage to get out between sobs.

My anger is directed at all of them. They all just watched and held her down, fucking cowards. They did it because their fucking leader told them to. He is the most disgusting of them all.

"Rain, what horrible things to say about your father, don't you think?" The deep voice is more casual now. It catches me by surprise.

Then I absorbed what he just said.

My father?

"My mother would never have gotten with anyone as fucked up and evil as you. You are not my father. I don't have a father!"

I scream with every ounce of air in my lungs into the room, it's high-pitched and full of pain.

My mother was just murdered, right in front of my eyes, and this piece of shit is alleging to be my father now, the leader of The Chapel.

"No need to say anything more. Let us finish the ceremony, and you can go back to your cell." He commands. He's upset that I am not welcoming him with open arms.

I am defeated. Alone. Heartbroken.

I just want to wake up. This can't be real.

Sobbing, my body goes limp in my handlers' hold. My head falls forward, and I am dazed, no longer able to focus or process what is happening.

The handler lets go of me, and my body falls hard to the ground. I'm sure it hurts, but I can't feel anything.

Unable to focus, I am caught by surprise when warm liquid touches my skin; still just in my thin sleep shorts and tee.

My vision gets distorted as they begin to pour it over my head, coating me as it runs down my fore-head, over my eyes and onto my lips. It drips to the ground in front of me. Opening my mouth slightly, I lick my lips. The taste of copper invades my tastebuds. The metallic smell creeps up my nose.

Another bucket gets thrown over me, coating the rest of my body.

It's blood.

Dark red, warm blood. At first, I think it's from an animal. I've heard of this, dousing people in pig or cow blood. But it's too warm, and too fresh. They would have had to have just slaughtered it.

Then a wave of realization washes over me.

This is my moms blood.

These monsters are draining her blood and coating me with it.

Sick sadistic bastards.

My father's voice commands the room once more, "With her blood, my daughter, my heir is reborn!"

I fucking hate him. I want to scream but can't.

The tiny drops that were once on the ground have turned into a large, crimson puddle surrounding me. I still don't move. Instead, I just stay here taking it. I need this to be over. If I fight, they'll take satisfaction in making me endure this longer.

Fingers begin touching my bare legs, arms and face. Blood drips off my lashes as I try to look around. I am completely surrounded by black cloaks now. My body is numb. My brain is protecting me now. I don't feel her anymore; despite being covered in her, my mom's presence was something extraordinary and now it is gone.

Faintly I begin hearing chants, none of this seems real. "Principessa Oscura, Principessa Oscura, Principessa Oscura..."

I'm not sure what it means. But I still feel *his* presence. Where is *he*? Why isn't *he* helping me?

"Take her back to her cell." His deep, commanding voice interrupts my thoughts.

Next thing I know, my body is being dragged, and

my heels are leaving a trail of blood behind me in the dirt.

"This bitch is slippery." One complains. It takes two of them this time, each holding one of my arms.

It doesn't take long for them to throw me back into my prison cell. The clicking of the lock shakes me out of the space I was in.

Looking down at my body, I see the familiar bat wings and an upside-down cross decorating my shirt. It was traced through the blood on my clothing.

Anything else that was traced on my skin has since been covered again. It's so thick and is starting to feel heavier on me as it drips off me. My hands reach up to my hair, it's soaked as well. I grip it in my hands and begin wringing out my disheveled ponytail.

My lip quivers and my chest heaves. I'm going to be sick.

They painted me with my mother's blood and left it on me to dry. The reminder is forever embedded in and on me.

I just want it off. Washing it off will help erase the memory of this horror. Using my short fingernails, I begin scraping my skin. Anything to get her blood off me. As it builds up with each drag, I wipe the excess off on the rocky walls surrounding me. I do this several times, but as it gets thinner, it begins to dry on my skin making it harder to remove. I desperately want to remove my blood-soaked, branded clothing, but I refuse to allow these fuckers to see me in my most vulnerable state, naked and imprisoned by them.

Curling into myself, my stomach turns as I move my body against the cool rock wall. Leaning on it, I let out one last scream of frustration. I scream until all the air is out of my lungs and my throat tingles.

Trying to keep it in doesn't work. Vomit follows, and I get sick next to where I am sitting, nothing more than bile comes out, as I haven't had anything to eat or drink in who knows how long.

Once it's all out, I let the tears dry on my skin. No use wiping them off.

My body continues to shake, it's exhausted, so I bury my face in my knees.

Closing my eyes, a vivid image flashes before me.

My father is the devil.

CHAPTER 6

ELIJAH

Rain was so sad, sitting there in front of us being doused in her mother's blood. She didn't hide her pain, she didn't fake her emotions.

If I were to guess what a broken heart looked like, she in that moment, is what I would imagine.

At one point, I felt like she had completely left us, her body was still there but her mind was gone. It was interesting to watch. How easily it was for her to disconnect from herself. Something about her has drawn me to her. Rain is one of the most interesting people I have ever laid eyes on. A curious creature.

Shy, but charismatic if she knows the person, like the regular at her work. Pale with long black hair and doesn't act like the typical chicks I am used to. She doesn't try to impress and is comfortable in her skin.

Or is she? I definitely caught every single glance she threw my way while I watched her work. Rain was curious, intrigued, but not scared.

Perhaps she craves more out of her life.

Since that night, where I spent her entire shift watching her, she is all I see. I need to know more about her. And if the old man keeps up his end of the bargain, I fucking will.

My curious little bat.

I made sure my bat wing tattoo was showing while lounging in the booth directly across from her, this way there was no mistaking where I came from. Blackwood, North Carolina, a member of The Chapel.

One thing did catch me off guard tonight. I didn't like the look on her face, she was completely devastated and broken.

I didn't like that.

I hate it actually, that she felt such pain. I never want her to feel that again.

When she saw her mother on the table, naked and held down by the other followers, as I stabbed my knife into her throat. As Rain screamed into the room and broke down crying, she was feeling pain. It bothered me. Then I noticed her detaching.

To me, it is just another body. Master, he gets names from their God, the Devil, whom they refer to as The Dark One. He is who they worship and who they do all of this for.

They have elected themselves those who rid the world of evil. Or who they perceive to be evil, who fucking knows, but that is a detail I couldn't give two shits about.

I am only here because my mom left my dad when I was ten and brought us here. Master, as he calls himself, is the leader of the highly rumored cult, The Chapel. He is also my stepfather, which technically makes Rain my stepsister. He quickly noticed my strengths and used them to his advantage. He's a fucking moron if he thinks I don't realize this.

Before me, they did hold killings and sacrifices, but not as often as they do now. The person before me didn't have an ounce of the skill I possess, he was sloppy and drew unwanted attention to The Chapel. He is swimming with the sharks now.

How it works now: Master spends hours and hours looking into the flames of a fire. This fire is lit around the clock, and followers will work in shifts to make sure of this. The fear is that if it ever goes out, then Master won't be able to communicate with their God anymore. Then their purpose could be compromised. Then, once he and The Dark One have spoken, he passes me a torn piece of paper with one name on it.

Each name I bring back to The Chapel has to land on La Notte del Diavolo, which loosely translated means Devil's Night.

Devil's Night is not scheduled. Whenever the fire gives a name, we begin the process.

We rid the world of what is evil towards The Chapel. We are out here doing our leader's work like the good little followers we are.

This time was unique, as I received two names. One to kill and one to keep, which is why I am here. I delivered both names, and now I want what is fucking owed to me. The one to keep was promised to me.

The sun will start to rise within the next hour, but that doesn't matter. My feet are propped up on his desk as I lean back in his expensive leather chair, playing and using my teeth to play with my lip piercing in his home office.

Rain Mills, my stepsister. She is fucking mine.

Although she will be a Sinclair soon, I am not letting her keep her dead mother's name. A smile forms on my face at the thought of it.

Rain Sinclair will be all fucking mine to do whatever I please. I'll own every single piece of her.

"What the fuck is on your face, boy?" Maxton Montgomery has entered the room. Our all-superior Master. I should add that I think he is a fucking fraud if you ask me, but his followers have been loyal to him for decades and I'm still alive, so I'm not about to call him out. Next thing you know, the bastard is handing me a piece of paper with my name on it. I think fucking not.

Looking up at him, "What does it look like?" I will not give him the satisfaction of a reaction that I frankly don't give a fuck.

For the past few months, I have had the darkest black around my eyes and on my nose. Then shading on my temples and the hallows of my cheeks, which each have a hard line leading to the corner of my mouth. Lines cross over the top and bottom of my lip. His question is that of a fucking moron. He knows what is on my face. Sometimes, the black paint does get itchy, but knowing how much he hates it makes me love it more.

Eventually, I will likely get my guy to ink it on me permanently. But until then, I am here for one thing: my prize.

Maxton rolls his eyes at me, "Feet off my desk. Move."

Not moving, I keep my eyes on him, "I'm not here to socialize with you. I am here to get what I am owed, then I will leave."

Maxton, who is in his dark dress pants and white dress shirt, which is unbuttoned with curly chest hair sticking out and pointed-toe fancy shoes, walks around the desk to face me. His hair is greased back. His eyebrows are basically one long eyebrow at this point. No wonder he has everyone in masks. I truly do not see what my mom saw in this guy. Must be a good fuck. Nothing else makes sense, as my dad paid her good money each month to take care of me. My dad is fucking loaded. So it has to be the dick.

Another reason for the white and gold masks with the long robes is that The Chapel requires full mandatory attire anytime they are in session, at the caves, so followers can never identify who else is there. They do speak, so they may recognize voices but never faces. Which is important when you're sacrificing people in the name of whomever they worship. Murder is illegal after all, if that sort of thing bothers you.

Maxton interrupts my thoughts, "Things have changed. He has spoken to me again since last night. After you killed her mother, the woman who stole her from us, The Chapel. I am going to keep Rain for myself. To create a pureblood heir to take over The Chapel when their time comes."

Liar.

I don't let my emotions show on my face. Keeping neutral, I question, "What about my mother?"

"She will understand. We cannot go against his wishes," he insists, dismissing my concern.

As Maxton speaks, I am picturing the many ways I could kill him right here, in his own office. Bashing his skull against the wall repetitively until pieces of his brain are stuck on his fancy wallpaper. Hold him down against the desk, mouth wrapping around the edge, while I stand on it. Then I would take my black steel-toed boot and step on the crown of his head until I heard his jaw break. But I wouldn't stop, I would keep going. The pain would cause him to pass out. As he lay on the ground, I would wait for him to wake up again, the pain would be excruciating, I imagine. I would take my number one choice, my baseball bat, and beat the living shit out of his head with it. How I desperately want to bash this motherfucker's head in. I have never liked him, and I'm sure I am the only one who sees through his shit. Everyone else who follows him is brainwashed and fooled by his charm. At this point, he could tell them he was just spoken to, that they must burn themselves alive, and they would fucking do it.

The restraint I have on myself right now is something he should appreciate.

Although just because I have restraint doesn't mean I am fucking happy about this.

"She is your daughter," I state, pointing out the obvious, which he seems to be ignoring.

He doesn't respond.

I cannot be bothered with his bullshit games right now. Getting up, I walk around him without saying a word before leaving. I am going to take what is fucking owed to me.

CHAPTER 7
ELIJAH

I haven't slept yet.

My blood is boiling as I speed down the dark backroads of Blackwood. My bright headlights are the only bit of light back here until the sun starts rising any minute now. Switching gears, my ignition roars louder as my speed increases. My dark hair is hanging over my forehead, and my nostrils flare with rage as my eyes focus on my destination ahead of me, The Chapel.

Blackwood is a small coastal town in North Carolina, which The Chapel has taken advantage of. The Chapel is located within one of the alcoves of the large rocky cliffs lining the coast. The cave's entrance is inland and has rooms branching out. If you walk straight through the long, dark and cold cave, it will take you to the sandy beach and ocean.

The locals don't come near this spot. My stepfather is widely known for running these parts.

I am positive most think he is absolutely unhinged, a notorious cult leader. The ones who don't are members, followers of him, and The Chapel. And once you're in, good luck getting out alive.

Over the years, people have whispered, and rumors have spread. Some are true, but they can never be proven.

When I get a name, good luck catching me. It will never fucking happen. So when someone goes missing, the town knows what has most likely happened. The police have learned to keep their distance. I was given one of their names once after they got too nosey into The Chapel's business.

Master claimed he was told, *'They must be taught a lesson.'*

The bodies are never found. How they are disposed of isn't up to us. Master tells us what has been decided and that is what we do.

It is convenient that we have an ocean nearby.

Do I believe his bullshit? No absolutely not, but I don't have enough energy to give a fuck. I get to do something I enjoy and I am the only one who has these privileges.

But that isn't the point. It doesn't fucking matter. This time I got two names. One to kill. One promised to me. Not to fucking him. I got them both out clean.

No one has a fucking clue. I killed her mom in front of her—not that it bothered me, but it clearly upset her.

She wasn't supposed to be upset!

If that motherfucker thinks he is going back on his promise, to take what's owed to me and what is mine. He is seriously more delusional than I thought.

Pulling up to The Chapel now, I noticed a few other cars are here as I shift gears and slam on the brakes. My car's tail end swings as my tires try to grip the loose gravel. It barely comes to a stop before I turn off the ignition and bolt out with my wooden baseball bat in hand, my vision is tunneled. I am here to do one thing, claim what is mine. She will never be fucking his. That's his goddamn daughter, for fuck's sake. I will not let him touch her.

Only ever me. Mine!

The thought makes my blood boil and my skin itch with fury.

My mind is forcing me to picture it. Him caressing her face with his fingers. Naked, she cringes but can't stop her nipples from hardening, it's cold in the caves. Rain will try to look away, but that doesn't put him off her. He grips her face, forcing her to look at him. He is seething as his other hand cracks against her skin. Her lip quivers—the reaction he craves. Then he forces two fingers between her lips, demanding her to suck them. Her eyes look up at him, pleading, hoping he will stop, but he won't. He can't.

A loud roar erupts from within me. My grip around the baseball bat tightens, and my fist is clenched as my knuckles whitten.

He will never touch her.

Gravel crunches underneath my black boots with each step. Entering The Chapel, fire from the torches are lit along the pathway, which causes my shadow to line one side of the wall. As I approach the holding cell area, I see one cloaked dickhead stationed outside of her cell. Stepdaddy must have called and warned that I would most likely be showing up.

And right he was.

Without saying a word, I walk towards him, there's no expression on my face as I begin twisting the bat in my hand.

"Elijah, you can't be back here. Master's orders." The smug fuck says to me.

He thinks he is important because he got orders from the all-seeing Master. He is nothing but a pawn like the rest of us, including me, but at least I know it.

I don't stop, continuing my ascent towards him and Rain.

Lifting my baseball bat up, I point it directly at him. I *tsk*, shaking my head. With his mask on, I cannot see his facial reaction, but if I were to guess, if he was smart, he should be shitting himself in fear.

If he isn't, then I am not doing my job properly. I

am Master's weapon, his killing machine, and this pawn is in my fucking way.

Today, this pawn decides to be brave instead of smart. He is so incredibly stupid, standing in defiance, blocking the archway opening to my Rain.

With one hand still gripping the wooden handle, I swing and it connects with his kneecap. His painful scream echoes, which only further pisses me off. If others are around, no doubt they will be coming this way soon. But I am not satisfied yet with my handy work, this fucker is still standing. So, I hit him once more, in the same spot. He drops like the useless pawn he is, screaming, "You fucking psychopath. You broke my knee."

His voice annoys me, so I swing again one last time, this time connecting with his head.

I don't put my full force behind it, killing him isn't of interest to me right now, but the force I do use knocks him out cold.

About fucking time. He needed to shut up.

Looking over to the cell, I see *her* sleeping, the commotion hasn't woken her.

Rain.

Stepping over the unconscious body, I walk up to the bars and take her in.

Dried blood still coats her from this past evening. She is curled tightly into a ball on the ground.

I've heard emotions tire people out, this is what

they must have meant. My eyes move up and down her body, taking every inch of her in.

I'm completely entranced by her. It's not like anything I have ever felt before. Something pulls me to her and makes me want to care about another person, about her.

Dropping my bat, I grab a hold of the steel bars. The flame in her cell casts dancing shadows on and around her, stunning.

"He won't let me have you. He promised me that you were mine. He fucking promised!" I rasp, shaking the bars.

"You are mine, little bat. Don't ever question it. Fucking mine."

A couple deep voices fill the silent space, shouting, "What's going on down here?"

"I will be back for you. I fucking promise. He won't have you."

She is breathing deeply, I can hear her inhale and exhale. Her body moves up and down with each, it is absolutely mesmerizing. I wonder if she is scared. Still sad, perhaps?

She is the most interesting creature I have ever seen.

I could watch her like this for hours, but I can't because *they* are coming. Fuck!

Letting go of the bars, I pick up my bat and head

back the way I came, which happens to be the same way the others are coming from. Convenient.

One appears in the open archway. I waste no time walking up to him and slam my bat against his skull. Nobody interrupts my time with my little bat. When will people learn? With this one, there is no opportunity for him to scream. Instead, he drops to the ground, his body limp and crimson blood splatters around us.

I smile. It's my favorite color.

Looking down, I step over the bastard. Dead or not, I don't care. He is out of my way.

Looking up, another peeks in and examines the area. He is smart because once he has taken the scene around him in, he holds his hands up in surrender. Very smart. Which is relatively shocking since this group is known for following.

Passing him, my body brushes against his. His gasp is audible.

Good. He should be pissing himself while thanking his merciful God that he lives to tell the tale of what he saw here today.

As I walk away down the dimly lit hall, I drag my bat behind me and I shout back, taunting him and whomever else may be lurking, "Go on. Call Master. Tell him what a very bad boy I have been. You have not seen shit yet, if a hair on her head is touched, you better hide."

I am coming back for you, little bat.

"Wake up, princess."

A loud feminine voice shouts at me, which wakes me from my sleep. My eyes are heavy and my body, which is still covered in dry blood, is feeling exhausted. Why can't they just leave me alone?

Slowly, I open my eyes, the torch is still lit and illuminating my cell. The steel door is open, with a single individual standing in the small opening.

"Get up." She snaps at me.

Like the others, she is dawning the long black robe, and a white mask with gold accents, with the hood over her head.

Laying on my side, I roll over slightly and place both hands on the earth next to me. I try to push myself up, which is harder than anticipated, and my muscles shake as I rise. It hurts, but I push through it, not wanting her to see how weak I am really feeling. I have a feeling that is the kind of shit they get off on.

The lady moves towards me and my heart races, panicking that I have upset her. Moving quicker, I push through the pain and exhaustion. I am on my hands and knees, as I start to rise. With the panic, my lip quivers as I see more of my mom's blood still on me. I can still picture them killing her. She couldn't escape, they held her down and pushed a blade through her throat. But she was strong until the end, not letting them see her scared, only strong. Which is what I need to be if I am going to survive this.

The lady moves out of the way of the opening and lets me pass her.

"Walk in front of me. Don't try anything, princess. I am authorized to punish you if you do." She threatens.

I nod in response and begin walking through the passage and hallways in front of her. She doesn't speak, only keeping her hand on my shoulder, guiding me where to go. As we walk into this larger space, it looks all too familiar to me. We are back where it all began.

Looking around the space, I notice the candles are lit, and the fire still roars, but not as many people fill the space this time. In the middle of the room is a large copper tub filled with water. My eyes then wander to where my mother was killed, it still has stained blood around the area.

I need to be strong, I cannot cry in front of these people.

"Principessa Oscura," my father greets me with his smug voice. Looking in his direction, he is also dressed like the others. I don't respond, instead waiting to hear what he has to say. The room is quiet.

"It is time for your cleansing, undress."

My face scrunches up with confusion. He must notice as he begins walking towards me, "Don't fight this. It will happen with or without your cooperation." He barks, echoing in the cave.

"How do I know you're telling the truth? That you are my father? I haven't even seen a picture of you before." I challenge him.

His bare hand reaches out and his fingers wrap around my neck, "How dare you question me? I am Master of The Chapel. The Dark One speaks to me. He told me where to find you and your evil, whore of a mother. Don't you ever forget the powers I hold here. Never fucking question me again. Do you understand me, daughter?" I can feel the rage with each word.

Looking up at him, I nod my head and whisper, "Yes, sir. I understand."

He lets me go, satisfied with my response but doesn't step back.

A cold object touches my skin, it sends a chill down

my spine. Looking down, he has a blade touching me, the tip of it is on my stomach where my skin is exposed.

"It is time for your cleansing, now fucking undress."

With shaking hands, I bring them to the hem of my shirt, which is stiff from the hardened blood embedded into each bit of fabric, up off my body. It crunches, then flakes as I continue to remove it and lift it over my head, exposing my bare torso and breasts. The shirt falls to the ground next to me as I move on to my sleep shorts. He doesn't move the blade.

Hooking my thumb under them, I begin pushing them down. Once I get them over my hips and bottom, they slide off on their own, bunching at my feet, leaving me in my lavender thong. Before I can reach to take them off next, his blade moves to just above the fabric covering my last bit of dignity. Goosebumps begin to rise all over my skin as my eyes watch the tip trace my skin, taunting me. My eyes look away, I can't watch this.

I can feel the blade move down my hip and my body tenses, preparing for the inevitable. Just as it does so, he brings the blade up and slices it through the fabric. He then moves to the other side and does the same.

I want to cover myself with my hands, but I won't give in. I won't let them get the satisfaction of thinking

I am embarrassed or ashamed. I'm not, I love myself and who I am. But they do not deserve to see me this way. He is a monster.

He grabs hold of my chin, forcing me to look up at him and asks, "Are you still intact?"

The question is puzzling, what does he mean intact? He must notice my confusion as he drops the blade to the ground and cups my pussy, repeating himself, "Are you still intact?"

I am mortified as my head shakes no in response.

Still cupping me, "Shame. Just like your mother. You won't be like her though, soon you will rule next to me. You have been given to me by the Dark One."

My eyes widen, and I react without thinking and spit on him out of disgust, "I will never. I would rather die." I declare, my voice is seething with rage.

He removes both his hands from my body, and within a blink of an eye, the back of his hand connects with my cheek. The force knocks me to the ground, and my dirty hair hangs over my face as I absorb what just happened. My eyes want to cry, but I won't let them. I will fight through this.

"Now get up and cleanse yourself. Wash away what remains of your mother and your tainted past. You will come out of the tub cleansed of it all and ready for the taking." He instructs.

I swallow, biting my tongue I want to scream. Fear is radiating inside of me but I listen, not wanting to make things worse. My feet move, one step at a time against the earth. I zone out the few followers surrounding the area, if I can't see them then they are not here watching me in my most vulnerable state.

Stepping over the ledge of the copper tub, I test the water with my toes, it is lukewarm so I lower the rest of my leg in and do the same with my other one. Placing both hands on either side for support, I lower myself down. Relief washes over me, this is exactly what I needed. As I am fully seated in the tub, I begin washing myself and the water turns red. Before I can move to my face and hair, I feel something cold on the top of my head followed by a set of hands, massaging it into my hair. It's him. My father. His scent is strong and musky. As uncomfortable as this is, it feels amazing so I don't move, instead letting him continue. Moments pass before his hands are off of me. I submerge myself under the water, using my own hands to rinse out the suds and wash my face.

Placing my hands back on the ledge, I rise. My hair is slicked back behind me as I open my eyes and gasp for air. I'm taken aback as I notice the followers have moved closer; they are surrounding me. My eyes take them in, none of them move or speak.

"Tomorrow you become ours, Principessa Oscura. Tomorrow, you will be prepared for the taking. Until then, you will remain in your cell. Now get up, dry off and change."

Nodding my head, I agree.

"Everyone out. Now!" My father demands of his followers. They obey without question, scurrying out of the room in single file.

"And after the taking, you will become my wife."

CHAPTER 9

RAIN

Wearing a black silk dress with thin straps over my shoulders, a plunging neckline and a high slit in the front that nearly exposes me. It has a slight train at the back, and a black upside down cross necklace around my neck and hanging between my breasts. My hair is down, and my feet remain bare as I walk into the main room.

It's just how it was the first night. All the followers are here, candles are lit and as I look over to the front, my father is standing there. My handler pushes me forward as we make our way through the crowd until we reach the table and stop just before it.

"Tonight we welcome Principessa Oscura to The Chapel, officially. Once the evening commences, she will be standing by my side as my new wife, in the name of the Dark One."

The room erupts, and they all chant back to him, "In the name of the Dark One."

A chill runs over me, not because I am impressed and moved by this performance and loyalty, it's because I am fucking terrified with no way out.

My father walks down the steps from where he is standing and walks to face me on the opposite side of the table.

"On the table," he insists. Accepting defeat, I do what he asks and pull myself onto the long wooden table, and lay in the same spot my mother did. Briefly, I hope I will feel her, considering this is where she had taken her last breath, but I don't. I feel nothing.

"Member Conrad, come forward. It is time to give her wings."

This is the first time I have heard a name being used. And wings? What is he talking about?

A hand wraps around my right wrist, holding it down so I can't move my arm. I wait for the same to happen to the rest of my limbs, but it doesn't. Instead, I hear a buzzing sound filling the quiet space. Glancing over, it's a tattoo machine.

I'm getting my bat wings.

The taking is The Chapel's initiation.

The needle pricks my skin as I look away. This is my first tattoo and it isn't a terrible pain, I actually like it. It's soothing—the sound of the buzzing machine and the needle pricking my skin. As I focus on that, time passes rapidly and the next thing I know, we are done. As he places his machine down and removes his black latex gloves, I take a peek. It is just like the one I saw on that guy at work. It looks like two wings are breaking out of my skin, just the outline and a bit of the inside are inked on me.

"Good job, Principessa Oscura. Now, let the taking begin." He shouts into the room and declares. Unsure of what is next, the hand wrapped around my wrist now moves my arm above my head. Another hand joins and does the same to my left arm. My father walks to the foot of the table and signals for a couple others to join him. As they stand with him, they take the fabric of my dress and rip the slit to my stomach, exposing me completely to them.

The taking.

It makes sense now. I am the one they are taking.

"Keep your eyes open. If they close, it will only last longer."

I want to scream. I want to fight. But it's of no use. There is only one of me against all of them, I wouldn't make it out of here alive if I tried.

A hand caresses my bare skin, moving slowly up my leg causing my toes to point and my body to stiffen. Just before the hand reaches my inner thigh, something changes.

I feel *him.*

He's here, but where? My eyes shift, trying to look around me without being noticeable. The feeling gets stronger with each passing second. Hope. I latch onto it, and I am not letting it go.

"Oh, stepdaddy dearest." A new voice taunts the room.

It's *him.*

My breathing becomes more rapid in anticipation. The room remains quiet. I want to move my head to see what is happening, but I resist. I don't need the attention back on me.

"Elijah, what is the meaning of your dramatics?" My father questions, unamused.

Elijah? I like that name.

"You gave her to me. I delivered both names to you on a silver fucking platter. After you promised me I could keep Rain! Now tell your goons to get their fucking hands off of her." His voice is dripping with venom.

"The Dark One has since changed his mind. This is not something any of us have control over, I am all but a vessel for him to communicate through."

I can hear footsteps getting closer. The connection feels stronger as *he* gets closer.

A million questions are racing through my head that I want to ask. That I want to scream about. But that isn't a priority right now; not getting raped by these vile human beings and staying alive is.

My eyes shift as I hear Elijah step next to me and stop. He is in all black, but not like the others, he has no robe, instead I think it's a hoodie. My eyes try to wander up where I see the shine of his piercings and his floppy black hair. Ink peeks out on his exposed neck, and he has some sort of markings on his face.

"The fuck did you do to your face?" Father shouts, and his voice echoes all around us.

Elijah doesn't respond. I see the corner of his mouth smirk. "If any one of you tries to stop me, I know where you live. I know where your kids go to school and what your spouses get up to while you are here. And I will kill them all without a trace if you fucking try to stop me." He says matter of factly.

My nostrils flare as my heart races. My body wants to tremble, but it takes every bit of willpower to prevent it. The adrenaline of not knowing what will happen next has hit me, fear and anticipation riddle through me.

Father is first to speak. "You have no idea what you are doing right now. How you will have to pay for this, Elijah. He will make sure you do."

"Would you shut the fuck up old man? I am not afraid of you or your Dark One. Pull my name next from the fire. It doesn't fucking matter to me." Elijah declares. As he does, I see his arm move up rapidly.

There is a wooden bat in his hand, which he slams down on the table just above my head.

My body jolts from the shock and loud noise.

"Get ready, little bat. We are going home."

I take that as my cue. It's time to move. Slowly I do, getting up with caution, unsure if someone will force me back down. Sitting up, my eyes take in the room. The followers are still surrounding us, observing what is happening before them. Elijah is challenging their Master, the vessel of their Dark One. And none of them are doing anything. Either out of shock or curiosity. Either way, I will take it.

"And mom, you are a fucking coward." He adds.

She must be in a robe and mask, as I cannot tell where she is. But surely she cannot be too pleased about her husband trying to take on another wife.

My dress is torn, exposing parts of me that I wish were not on display. As I get off the table, I grab the torn pieces and try to tie a couple of them together quickly to limit the vulnerable feeling that has taken over me.

Once I do, I look up to see the most beautiful set of eyes looking back at me. They are blue with specks of brown in them. Enchanting.

His face is decorated with black ink, like a skeleton. The black bits around his eyes, nose and temples are all shaded, leaving the rest of his skin exposed. His mouth has black lining on and around it. As I continue to examine him, I know he won't hurt me. The trust is instant and unspoken. His energy speaks to mine, which is enough for me.

Elijah reaches out his free hand, and I take it. Instantly, my body buzzes as if it weren't alive until now. A fresh wave of energy ignites inside of me. I feel connected to him in ways I have never felt before towards another person.

Looking at his other hand, the bat is now hanging in his grip, the wood has a slight chip in it and is stained red. My eyes move back to my father, and the followers who were up until recently were touching me, but I didn't say anything. I refuse to give them any more of me, they do not deserve it.

"Little bat, we can go now. They won't hurt you," Elijah coaxes me, and his thumb rubs the top of my hand. I nod in response, refocusing on him.

"Follow us, and you're dead. Try to find us, dead..." My father interjects, "We get it. Your childish games and antics will catch up to you. The Dark One rules within you as much as it does me."

"No one rules me, but me. I humor you. Remember that."

Elijah starts to walk away, pulling on my hand and bringing him with me. We don't make it far before I hear someone rushing behind me. It all flashes before me quickly. Elijah, without letting go of me, maneuvers himself so he is now in front of me. His arm, along with the bat, is in the air before it comes down with full force, connecting with the person's head.

You can hear the impact, gasps of shock fill the area.

"Your family will be dead before you get home tonight. I will make sure you find them."

The person on the ground hasn't moved. Unsure if they are dead or alive, Elijah turns and continues walking us out. The followers part for us, clearing a path to the exit. As we walk through the long hallways, neither of us speaks. A part of me is unsure if this is real or if I have become delusional. Either way, I will take it.

A black car is parked at the entrance, engine still on.

Elijah walks me to the passenger side and opens the door for me. I get in and he closes the door behind me. I do up my seatbelt and curl into myself on the seat as he gets in. As we begin to pull out of the area, it's dark and hard to tell where we are. Both of us stay quiet as we make our way down the backroads, the only thing lighting the area are his headlights. Then unexpectedly, his hand grips my knee and says, "Little bat, you are mine now."

ELIJAH

My home is located outside of Blackwood, surrounded by thick woods for privacy. My dad, who still doesn't get why I haven't come back to Montana yet, comes from money, therefore, I come from money. I've not returned because I know I will end up there soon enough. This is my last taste of absolute freedom before then.

My place isn't anything massive. A three thousand square feet, single-story bungalow on four acres of land is a fortress with a state-of-the-art security system throughout the property, inside and out. If any motherfucker tries to come up uninvited, they won't be around to tell the tale of what happened. The town knows not to bother me; they know what I do for The

Chapel and the last time a cop got involved, his name was given next. That shit was not a coincidence.

It was that moment when I truly knew my stepfather was full of absolute shit, along with his delusional followers. Anything to justify what they do. I collected the names regardless, and on La Notte del Diavolo, devil's night, I killed them.

Killing doesn't bother me along with most things in life. I have been told my emotions aren't human, or the lack thereof. I know what I want and what I like, and I will do anything to get to it once I have my mind set. Some say it is hyper-fixation, I call it passion and determination. And that is what Rain is. My passion and determination. And now I have her. She is home. She is fucking mine.

We haven't spoken since getting here. Once arriving, I lead her to my bathroom, where I leave her to shower and change. I stay in the bedroom, on the floor with my back against the closed bedroom door, unable to leave her side. She comes out of the bathroom in a pair of my sweats and a sweater, which are baggy and hanging on her petite frame. Rain's dark hair is still damp, with her eyes puffy and face blotchy. My eyes examine her, trying to sort out what is wrong. Rain's eyes glisten as she looks back at me, but they also seem vacant. Why is she sad? She's home. I rack my brain trying to figure out what is happening. The only conclusion I have is that I don't like when she's feeling this way.

No words are spoken even then.

Instead, she makes the first move, walking over to the bed and gets herself under the covers. Within minutes, her breathing is heavier.

Rain is still asleep, and I haven't left this spot in the room since. Listening to her inhale and exhale is relaxing. Her presence soothes me. I noticed that when I sat in the bar she worked at. It's something I haven't felt before, peace.

Looking at my phone, it's been nearly eight hours. The sun has risen, and some of it tries to creep through the blinds to light the room. I'm not tired, I could sit here forever, listening to her and protecting her.

The bedsheets move, catching my attention. Rain's tired voice follows, "How long have you been sitting there?"

"Since you went for your shower."

She doesn't respond right away. Moments have passed before her next words come out, "Why?"

"It's my job to protect you, to make sure you're always safe." I respond, confused by her question. How could she not understand that mine means mine in all ways, and I take care of what is mine.

Rain sits up to look at me, her hair is disheveled, but her face looks rested, "Then it's my job to take care of you. You need your rest too if you are going to be my savior."

An uncomfortable feeling erupts in my chest. It's nothing I have felt before, and I'm not sure what it means. But not a day in my life has anyone taken care of me, or even wanted to. My parents were always in their own worlds. My dad was always busy with work, gone for days at a time. He loved me and still does, but our relationship isn't typical. My mother on the other hand, resented my dad and used alcohol, pills and other men's dicks to fill that void. Which is how we ended up here.

And now I have Rain, and she wants to take care of me?

She pats the spot on the bed next to her, "Come on. You need to sleep."

Nodding, I stand up and toe my boots off. I check the bedroom door once more, making sure it's still locked. I am not paranoid, I am smart. I just pissed off a lot of fucking people by taking her and challenging Master.

Walking over to the bed, I drop my bat to the ground. It crashes against the hardwood and rolls slightly. Getting in under the covers, Rain lowers herself back down to her pillow. Her hands are under her head, and she is rolled over facing me, as I face her. We don't speak, our eyes take each other in, examining each eyelash and freckle.

"Why do you want to take care of me?" I need to understand, because I don't get it.

Her lashes brush against her pale skin with each blink. "I feel you before I even see you. It's a connection you protect, you hold on to and take care of. I barely know you, but I need you. I feel safe with you. I knew you were coming to help me." She explains.

"I killed your mom. And I don't feel bad about it. I never feel bad about it. None of them mattered."

Her eyes squeeze shut, and tiny lines form around them as a faint whisper leaves her parted lips, "I know." A couple tears stream down her cheeks as she continues, "I felt you then. I knew you were there, but I wasn't sure where. The worst thing to ever happen to me was that night, losing my mom and knowing now you were responsible for it. Logic is screaming at me to run. My mom is whispering to me to stay. She is telling me my gut isn't wrong. They used you to do their bidding, the coward couldn't even kill her himself. His Dark One didn't give her name. She is the most selfless person. He wanted her gone. But then you came back. You saved me. You won't hurt me. I know you wouldn't."

My expression remains unchanged as I try to absorb what she is telling me.

"I don't care that they use me. I like it, hurting and killing people. But I also know your father is full of shit. I've known for years. His day is coming, and the timeline has moved up. But you are right on one thing, I would never fucking hurt you on purpose. Unless it was during sex."

My last addition makes her giggle. I like seeing her like this, even if sadness is still in her eyes.

"What's your last name?" She asks.

"Sinclair."

Nodding her head. "I'm going back to sleep. Now close your eyes," Rain instructs. Oh silly little bat, trying to boss me around, I will let it slide this one time.

Then she catches me off guard, leaning forward, her lips brush against mine. My hand reaches up and grips the back of her head as I deepen the kiss, and my tongue brushes against hers as electricity ignites inside of me. This girl makes me fucking feral, I want to devour her. But not yet. She needs her rest. I let go of her and kiss her once more before pulling back. She doesn't move, her eyes remain closed and her breathing becomes heavier. Her eyes open slowly as her hand touches my face, her thumb rubs against my bottom lip a couple times before she pulls away, lays her head back down and closes her eyes. My heart could very well jump out of my chest at any moment. The need to possess her and keep her has only grown. She can never leave now.

Once I am sure she is asleep, I whisper, "Take care of my soul, it's yours now."

CHAPTER 11
ELIJAH

I woke up after a couple hours of restless sleep. I've been keeping myself busy with plans for tonight, it's dark out now and the day is gone. Rain is still passed out, the girl can fucking sleep. She's been asleep for nearly twenty-four hours. But I need to wake her, we have things to do and I am not leaving her alone.

After my shower, I changed into my black jeans, black hoodie and combat boots, my standard outfit on most days. I have my hood over my head as I admire the new ink on my face in the mirror. It's fucking perfect.

Looking at my phone it's nearly midnight, we have to get moving. I leave the bathroom and walk up to my sleeping Rain. "Little bat, you have to get up. We have places to be."

It takes some effort, but eventually I am able to coax her out of her sleep.

"E, I'm tired. Let me sleep," she moans. This girl is going to kill me. She could fold me ten ways to Sunday.

"Little bat, you have been sleeping for a day. You need to get up and we have to go."

Walking over to the floor lamp, I turn it on, which makes her immediately react like she is a vampire allergic to the light. The blankets move over her head as she continues to moan, "No. Please don't make me, your bed is so comfortable."

"Our bed and I don't care, so get up," I say as I pull the blanket off of her. "I got you some clothes delivered. They are on the dresser. I will give you privacy to change, I will be out there." I point over my shoulder towards the door. She doesn't say anything back, instead just glaring at me, which doesn't bother me. She will quickly learn.

I leave the room, closing the door behind me and head down the hall into the living room. Sitting on the plush black sectional, I kick my feet up on the coffee table and wait. A loud scream comes from where I had just left, but it doesn't alarm me. I know exactly what she has just seen on top of the clothes I left behind.

As I continue to wait, I hear the bedroom door open and her feet walking on the wood floors. Rain bursts into the room, but I don't turn to look.

"What the fuck is this?" I can only assume what

she is waving around is her new driver's license and passport, which I had made for her the same night I took her. I had my guy take care of everything.

"What does it look like?" I casually ask, not bothered.

"Sinclair? Rain Sinclair?"

Finally, I look over and I can see she is in the clothes I left for her—a matching black hoodie to mine, black leggings with black boots. Her hair is down and she has a scowl on her face. Fucking gorgeous.

"Did I stutter when I said you were mine?" We really don't have time for this.

"You are unbelievable. You can't just change my name without asking." She sounds defeated now, knowing she isn't going to win.

"I already have. Perhaps in the future, should I want to consult you on these things, I will." I'm not sure what more she wants from me at this point.

"As much as I want to have this back-and-forth shit. We have somewhere to be." I say as I stand up from the couch.

"Where are we going?"

I don't respond, instead heading towards the front door. I open the keypad next to it and enter the security code, which is needed whenever I leave. It gives me five minutes to leave before reactivating the entire system. Then opening the door, I look over at Rain and

she takes the hint, putting her new license and passport down on the front entrance table before walking
out to the lit driveway and gets into my car parked out
front. I close the door behind me and follow.

It's time to teach my little bat how to hunt.

Rain Sinclair hasn't spoken to me the entire fifteen-
minute drive into Blackwood. My headlights are off
now as I pull up on the street where that fucker from
the other night lives. I promised his family would be
dead for him to find, and I don't make fake promises.
Not doing it last night after getting Rain was due to
two things, I needed to get her home, rest was my first
priority and secondly, I wanted him to feel safe.

I wanted him to feel like he won, like he was a
fucking king who lived to tell the tale.

This stupid motherfucker has a wife who resents
him and a son who is a twenty-nine-year-old fucking
pervert. Who also lives at home still. On any given
night, you can catch him peeking through windows
and watching people. He isn't picky about gender or
age. Recently, a male senior reported seeing him
through his bedroom window. The police couldn't do
shit considering who his dad is associated with. But I
can and will. And tonight, my little bat is going to start
learning she can too.

Parking, I turn off the car as Rain breaks the silence.

"What are we doing here?" She whispers.

My head falls against my headrest as I blow out a breath. "He isn't home. I promised he would find his family dead. This is me keeping that promise. You are going to help me, sister."

As I finish speaking, I look over to her and she doesn't react, interesting. Perhaps she is instead taking it all in?

I am not sure if I'm fully honest as I've never had this conversation with another person before.

"Where's my mom's body? What did they do with her?"

"Typically, they feed them to the sharks. But I had her moved and buried on our property. This way you can visit her whenever you want. I didn't know what else to do. You were so sad, and I..." Before I can finish, Rain cuts me off, whispering, "Didn't they question you?"

Shaking my head, "No, because I told them I would handle the body before the ceremony. They have no idea."

We sit in silence until I start tapping the steering wheel with my fingers.

Her tiny voice appears again.

"Thank you."

I don't respond. There is no need to.

Looking over at the house, the lights are off and I can tell the window on the side of the house is open, as it usually is.

"Once I get in, I will open the front door for you. Not a fucking sound once you enter. Follow my lead, and do not question me. I do this a lot more than you would want to know about. I know what I am doing, and I don't need any pointers or someone questioning me. Do you understand?"

Her eyes burn into mine as she nods in understanding.

Rain puts her hair up in a ponytail, ready to go.

Good little bat.

CHAPTER 12
RAIN

Most people would think I was the biggest moron.

A part of me would agree with you. Staying with the boy who kidnapped me and then hand-delivered me to the devil, who is my father. Trusting the boy who killed my mom. And who I think is about to kill this family. But deep in my soul, I know this is right. He is where I am supposed to be. My mom would agree, he is my safe place now. Our connection is undeniable.

It's something that is hard to explain, and no one but us would ever understand. Since the first day at the bar. He feels it too, I can tell. Some may think he is over-the-top protective, but I think it is so perfectly him. Just like the tattoo decorating his face.

He is beautiful.

I feel a slight smile form on my face, my muscles are confused. They haven't moved in days to show any expression other than sadness. It feels nice to smile.

Then I think back to how he already knew I was his. Arranging for my mom to be buried on his property, to keep her close to me. So I can visit whenever I want. He knew then that I was his. That he was going to keep me. Which helps keep the smile painted on my face as my head turns to face the passenger-side window.

My eyes wander towards the direction of the house I am still sitting in front of. I am waiting in the car while Elijah breaks into the house, it would be suspicious if I were to wait out front for him. It's a peaceful evening, the moon is out and the stars are shining.

Before I let my eyes wander any further, I see the silhouette of Elijah at the front door. My eyes blink and that's all it takes, he is already gone. That's my cue.

Getting out of the car, I walk casually across the street to not look suspicious and up the front pathway to the unlocked door. Opening it, I slide in quickly and then close it shut behind me. It's dark, my eyes are still adjusting as I step forward, walking into a hard body, Elijah. I'm taken back, stumbling before finding my balance again. As I do, he takes my hand into his, and turning around he leads us down the front hall, which leads to the bedrooms. We pass a bathroom, then reach a closed door. He squeezes my hand once. To reassure me and to remind me. Follow his lead.

He lets go of me and slowly begins to open the closed door. My heart is racing, at any moment this door could squeak and the person on the other side would wake, becoming aware of our presence. Elijah though, he is calm and not phased by the lingering *what-if's*. The moon's light shines through the window, and my eyes move around the room as I follow Elijah in, it's the master suite. One body lays in the bed, sleeping peacefully. Completely unaware of the unpeace about to occur.

Elijah walks up to the side of the bed, barely acknowledging the person before him as he reaches out and covers their mouth. As I walk closer, I can see it's her, the man's wife from the night before. Her eyes open in panic after feeling his touch against her skin. Before she is able to panic, Elijah steps ahead, his hand is already at her throat, slicing it open ear to ear with a sharp blade. Muffled cries escape her, he is the last person she will see, all because of her husband. I wonder why she stayed. Why not leave this shitty fucking town and start over?

It doesn't matter now.

Her fingers scratch at Elijah while he continues to apply pressure on her face, keeping her still and silent. Her efforts weaken with each movement. As I watch, it takes a minute, maybe two for her body to become lifeless. Her feet have stopped kicking under the sheets, and her hands have stopped scratching. She is dead.

I don't feel bad. She married a monster. Guilty by association for staying.

She fucking knew.

Elijah removes his hand from her, puts the blade, still coated with blood, in his pants pocket and turns to face me. I nod, reassuring him that I am ok. He doesn't respond, instead he grabs my hand again and leads us out of the room.

We step back into the hall. The door across from us is also closed. He steps up to it, looks back at me and whispers, "This one's yours."

CHAPTER 13
ELIJAH

As the words leave my mouth, I can feel her body tense up.

This is our life. No better way to learn it than to be thrown into it. It's how I learned from my dad, but I wanted to. He knew I needed it. My body craved having the ability to take a life in as many ways as I could. To kill just one way would get boring, but having options kept the fire inside of me alive. Based on the person, I would pick the perfect approach.

I imagine this is a life she has not thought of until recently. Although, it is one she will come to enjoy. She is here because she wants to be. Rain could have run away when I left her alone in the car. But that's not her. She wants to be freed and I am the one to free her, allow her to spread her fucking wings and become the woman her soul craves to be, beside me.

My little bat is free.

Opening the door, I lead us into the room of the sick mother fucker. He is snoring and sleeping on his single bed. Turning around, I hold my finger up to Rain, and she nods in understanding.

This fucker is going to be awake for everything, he doesn't deserve quick like his mom.

Walking up to the side of the bed I slap his face, once, twice, and then a third time.

"Fuck you doing?" He shouts with sleep still in his voice.

Bending over, so my face is close to his, I whisper, "Killing you."

He startles, begins to panic and tries to get off his bed. He isn't a small guy, so the entire bed shakes with each movement. Growing tired of his dramatics and creating a little distance, when his head rises off the pillow, I punch him in the temple, knocking him out cold. As he falls back, I am already moving to the foot of the bed, throwing off his blankets, and grabbing his bare ankles. He is only wearing boxers, by the looks of it.

Pulling him out of bed, I start to drag him onto the floor. Rain steps aside so I can continue out of the bedroom and down the hall, she follows. It is still dark inside, the moon is the only thing lighting the area. As we reach the end of the hall, where the kitchen and living room are open to each other, I drag him to the middle of the area and leave him there.

Walking up to Rain, I take her hand, open her palm and place the same blade I just used into her hand. It is not the one I used on her mom, this is one from my own personal collection and perfectly sharpened for this evening.

As I close her fingers around it, I take her in. I cannot wait to see her destroy him, taking out everything that has happened these past couple days on him.

Looking down at her, I grip her face and smash my lips against hers, taking and devouring anything that she will give me. This is the last time she will be this version of herself. Because in five minutes, she will be a new person.

A killer, just like me.

I nip her lip, then lick it with the tip of my tongue, where I can taste the copper coming from. Fucking delicious. I could devour her like this until the end of time but not here, not now. Breaking our kiss I step back, she doesn't lick her lips to clean up any blood. Instead, she lets it be, I hope I bit hard enough so some trickles down her chin.

My mind goes back to the other night, she was covered in her mom's blood from head to toe. It dripped off her body and pooled around where she was sitting. A fucking goddess.

My cock strains against my pants at the thought.

Stepping aside, I encourage her, "When he wakes up, don't let that scare you. This is the one time I will tell you to make it as messy as you can. He is a fucking pervert, and his dad deserves to have what you and I have done here embedded in his brain forever. Do you understand?"

Rain takes a deep breath in before responding, "I won't let you down."

I wish I could take my dick out now and stroke it while she is killing this mother fucker. There is nothing stopping me but this is her first, it's best I don't distract her. But fuck, I have never been this turned on before. I am aching with need.

She has come to trust me so easily, like we have known each other forever. It's dangerous and dumb, but then what does that make me? We are both fucked.

I rub my cock from the outside of my pants and blow out a deep breath. The power she has willingly given me—not that I needed more, but fuck. To possess it from her is exhilarating.

Walking closer to the bastard on the floor, I kick him in the side of his ribs a couple of times with my boot, "Wake the fuck up."

His eyes flutter as he grabs his side, "What do you want? Take it, it's yours."

"We are," I promise while looking down at him. Suddenly he is fully alert, which happens once they realize what is about to happen.

I look up at Rain and slightly nod my head. Before she begins, I step on this fucker's face, putting all my weight on that leg. His screams of pain are slightly muffled as I speak to him once more, "If you try and fight us, *her*, the more it will hurt. We already want you to hurt, and promise, it will fucking hurt. But I can make it worse."

Adrenaline is flowing through my veins. This is my favorite part. Good or bad, I couldn't give a fuck, playing with my prey before finally ending them is what feeds me. Knowing my little bat is about to do this for the first time satisfies me just the same.

Rain steps closer, with the blade in hand. She reaches out over his pelvis and her hand shakes, nerves. She cannot be hesitant, she needs to be confident.

"Just do it. Don't think. Let your instinct take over," I encourage her.

Lowering herself to the ground next to him, she gets on bent knees, and her free hand pulls his boxers down, exposing his tiny penis and oversized balls. As the realization of his situation hits him, he begins moving more, his arms move to try and feel where Rain is as his hips move side to side. Thankfully Rain is not within reach, if he were to even brush her with a fingertip I would curb stomp the fuck out of his head. Breaking his skull with the bottom of my boot would bring me great fucking pleasure.

The thought enrages me.

No one fucking touches her but me.

"I will break your jaw right fucking now if you don't stop moving." I threaten through gritted teeth.

It takes every ounce of self-control to not just end him now from the thought of it.

Taking my mind off it, or at least trying to, I focus back on Rain, "Little bat, if you don't do something while on your knees, I will make use out of your current position."

She looks up at me, licking her lips then winks as she grabs ahold of the fuckers giant balls. Cheeky bitch. Fuck, I am lucky.

Rain positions the blade against his balls and with one fluid motion, cuts through the thin sack skin. Blood trickles down her fingers and she continues to cut them off. My eyes fixate on her, so fucking beautiful. As she makes the final slice, she leans back on her heels holding the detached, bloody ball sack in her hand. Pride shines across her face as she looks up at me for approval.

"Little bat, you did so fucking good." I praise. Her smile grows even bigger across her delicate face.

She places the appendage next to her and moves to

his tiny cock. As she grips it, her face shrivels in disgust but that doesn't stop her. Doing the same thing she did to his balls, she slices clean through it. Faintly I can hear his scream, but I am too focused on Rain to be aware of how loud he is being.

Instead of placing his cock with his balls, she keeps it in her bloody hand. Looking up at me, "He is being too loud. Let me shove this in his mouth."

I am bending her over and fucking her bare here once we are done.

Keeping my foot on his head, I bend at the waist and grip the sides of his head, "You are annoying my little bat. Open your mouth and accept her gift, it will help you shut the fuck up."

His eyes glisten in the moonlight, the bastard is crying like the little bitch he is.

Immediately after I remove my foot from his face, an excruciating scream leaves his mouth. This mother fucker doesn't listen. Moving my thumbs to his eye sockets, I push as hard as I can while whispering into his ear, "I told you to stay fucking quiet. Now shut the fuck up and let my girl shove your tiny cock into your annoyingly loud mouth before I push your perverted eyes through your thick but empty skull."

I can feel the tears under my thumbs, pussy, as his mouth opens. Drool runs down his chin as he whimpers. Rain moves forward and shoves the bloody cock into his mouth. He gags as blood joins the stream of drool. I pull back from his eyes and place one hand under his chin, forcing his head back and closing his mouth. I place my other hand over his nose. "If you keep moving and moaning, I will plug your nose and suffocate you. Have you die by choking on your own cock, do you want that?"

He shakes his head in defeat, still crying like a fucking baby.

Rain has already moved on, and her blade traces along his arm, "What did he do? You're making this one last longer." Very observant little bat.

"He is a fucking pervert, little bat. He needs to feel the pain. He isn't good."

She looks back at me, head slanted. "Neither are you."

"You're right, I'm not. Now you aren't either, babe."

She takes a moment to absorb what I just said, not moving or taking her eyes off of me. Her head slowly begins to nod as she whispers, "Everything has changed. This is my new life now."

As the words leave her mouth, the blade pierces his skin and she moves it up his arm. She has cut his radial artery, the one most people cut in the wrong direction, but not her, she did it right. Blood begins to rush out of his wrist and arm, puddling around her knees. He only has a few minutes left now.

Moving quickly, she isn't wasting time. As she

positions herself next to his head, across from me she spits, "Break his jaw." I look into her eyes, the thrill of the kill has taken over. Rain is gone, and my little bat is fully present.

I stop applying pressure to his jaw. I let his head lower before placing my fingers inside his mouth, on either side. I cup the rest of my hand around his chin and the other over his nose and pull with all my force in opposite directions until I feel the pop and hear the crack. What a fucking rush!

The tiny penis flops out of his now dangling jaw onto the floor next to me.

Little bat drops the knife next to her, we both move, meeting over him as he continues to bleed out, and mouths collide.

I am already grabbing her shirt and pulling it up her body. We part briefly as I pull it over her head, throwing it to the side. She isn't wearing a bra, fuck me. I join her, standing up, I remove my own hoodie and walk to be on the same side as her.

"This isn't going to be gentle. I am going to fuck your tight cunt until you're screaming my name, little bat. My dick has been hard since you took the blade, he needs to be inside you."

She giggles at my claim, but I am not playing little bat.

My cock continues to strain against my pants as I position myself behind her.

I move my hands, finding her waistband and pull her leggings down past her perky ass and leave them at her knees.

"Place your hands on the other side of this fucker," I instruct, and she obeys.

As she positions herself over his face, I move the thin thong fabric to the side and with two fingers, brush against her dripping pussy. Her breath hitches as her back arches.

"If you fucking look at her tits, I will make your death last longer." I threatened him. He doesn't respond.

I tease her a couple more times before I stop and begin to undo my belt, then my pants. I pull them down, freeing my throbbing cock. I grip it tight as I move closer behind her, guiding him slowly inside. She moans, "Fuck." Under her breath. Her pussy is like a vice, gripping me instantly.

My cock ring rubs against her walls.

Then, grabbing her shoulder with my free hand, I slam myself hard inside of her.

I warned her this wouldn't be nice.

Another moan escapes her as she throws her head back, sending me into a frenzy. Looking around us all we see is, blood, bodies and raw fucking passion.

She is never leaving me.

I continue to thrust into her, my pelvis pounding against her skin as we both take what we need.

"Such a good fuck toy for me, aren't you?"

She doesn't respond.

"Such a bad fucking girl. Ignoring your brother as he fucks your tight, needy cunt."

I feel her pussy tighten around my cock. My heart is racing as the familiar tingling sensation builds.

"Elijah, it feels so fucking good. Take it all. Use me. Destroy me. I'm yours." She pants.

That does it. Ropes of my come begin to coat her walls. I work her harder and faster, addicted to this feeling. I never want this moment or this connection to end.

I continue to fill her with my come as her own orgasm takes over, her pussy milks my cock as she coats me with her release. I take my hand and slap her ass as I pound into her from behind. Her skin cracks against mine, and her back arches further as another moan leaves her. I want my marks all over her.

Letting go of her shoulder, I grip her throat, needing to leave a mark there too.

Our movements slow down, and I squeeze her around the neck once more before letting go. Her head lowers as she catches her breath. My heart is racing, I can hear it beating in my ears. I have never had sex like this. Over a dying person, well most likely already dead now, and to come by just being inside of her.

"You are never fucking leaving me. Do you understand?" I ask her as if I want her to respond, but I don't.

She turns her head over her shoulder, panting and looking at me confused, before she whispers, "Never."

Pulling out of her, my cock is dripping with our mixed release. I tuck myself back inside my pants and stand up, allowing her to lean back and pull her own pants up.

Walking over to the other side, I grab both our tops and pass her one as I put mine back on.

Breaking the silence, "Elijah, get me a knife from the kitchen, please." She asks me in a sex daze, and I obey.

My boots squeak against the floor from the wet blood on them. I open a couple drawers as I enter the space, looking for the sharp knives. Finding one, I grab it, walk it back over and hand it to her. Taking it, she uses it to point towards the tiny penis next to me. Bending down, I grab it and pass it to her.

Little bat places it on the pervert's bare chest, and then with both hands wrapped around the handle of the blade, she drives it into him, pinning the penis in place. He doesn't scream or move.

The fucker is dead. This place is a mess. Perfect for how I wanted that prick to find it once he gets home.

The last thing he will do is ask the police to investigate.

He will know I did it. He will know I could do it to him. Fingerprints don't worry me.

Rain picks up the blade I brought from the thickly pooled blood and passes it to me, still dripping. Not giving a fuck, I shove it in my pocket and start to walk toward the front door. "Let's go little bat, our work here is done."

CHAPTER 14

RAIN

Laying in bed, I can't sleep.

Realization of tonight's events hit me while I was in the shower. Elijah, if he has noticed, hasn't said anything. He is different though, the emotions I feel are foreign to him. No remorse, no sadness and at times, no logic. He has his own way of thinking and dealing, it seems to be working, so who am I to judge.

I keep reminding myself and convincing myself that the followers of The Chapel are vile people. The members of their family we just slaughtered deserved it. They condoned this bullshit. Whoever he is, was going to do unimaginable things to me that night if E didn't come and get me.

Wherever I close my eyes, it's all I see. The blood—

so much fucking blood. The muffled screams of terror fill my head.

Suppress, suppress, suppress.

I say silently to myself.

Being good for twenty-one years has gotten me nowhere.

They deserved it. If we hadn't done it first, they would have done it to us.

Don't confuse this with remorse. It's not that. It is me coming to terms with what happened tonight. Embracing the new me, the true me.

With each cut of the knife, a euphoric feeling radiated through me. I fucking loved it. I finally felt fully satisfied. Elijah knew that this was what I needed. I don't know how, but he's known all along. Since that first night in the bar. Our connection, our need for one another. My energy feeds off his and vice versa. This is something unbreakable, and even the thought of someone trying terrifies me. No one can separate us.

Then my mom enters my thoughts. Fuck, I need her right now.

Trust him. He is loyal to you. He is strong for you. You are safe with him. He would never let anything happen to you. And you wouldn't allow it toward him. Trust your gut and your heart. Never second-guess it. Not with him.

Elijah's phone starts to ring, breaking me out of my thoughts. I look over at him. His black hair has fallen over his forehead, he is at peace sleeping. Beautiful.

The phone continues to ring as he comes to life, mumbling something under his breath. Rolling over, he feels for his phone on the bedside table until finally finding it.

Answering it, he puts it on speaker, he knows I am awake.

"What the fuck did you do?" My father shouts through the speaker.

E blows out an annoyed breath. "You woke me to ask me a stupid fucking question? You know exactly what I did."

"You little shit. You ungrateful bastard. Do you know how much this is going to cost me to cover up?"

"I have a dad, thanks. And just threaten to pull one of their names from your magical fire. That should scare the police chief enough. I warned that prick what I would do. None of this should be a shock." Elijah chuckles back.

"That is my number three you have fucked with. Don't think you will get away with this. Major consequences are coming. Make sure you come to Chapel tomorrow night. And bring the girl you stole from me." My father demands. Hatred is seething with each spoken word.

Elijah doesn't respond, instead ending the call and placing his phone back on the table. He rolls over to face me when I ask him, "Why do you still call me little bat? I don't want to be that anymore. I am not my father."

He brings his hand to my cheek and caresses it. "But you are. You grew your wings, embraced the dark and joined me in the night. We take the blood, drink it and bathe in it. It feeds us, our souls. You are always my little bat."

Chills flow over my body as he speaks.

"This was your first. I will give you tonight off. You better be out of your head by the morning. We have our own names to pull from the fire, little bat." I nod in understanding. It's spooky how in my head he is. But comforting. I don't need to speak, he just knows.

Removing his hand, he pulls me closer to him. I wrap my leg around his and that's how we both fall asleep.

Waking up, the sun is shining brightly into our room. Elijah is gone. Looking towards the bedroom door, it's open. I panic. Where is he? He has never left me alone.

I get up wearing only one of his tees, which is over-sized on me and pad out of the room to the living room, where I found him last time. But it's empty; he isn't on the black plush sectional, the television on the wall is off and the entire house is oddly quiet. As I walk towards the kitchen, which is off to the other side of the house from the front entrance, something through the large back windows catches my eye.

Large orange flames are coming from the yard. Surrounded by gray rocks to contain it. Walking up to the window, I look around the yard to try and find E. What is he doing?

A loud noise comes from behind me—the front door slamming, which makes me jump out of my skin. Turning around, my eyes wide and scared, Elijah is standing in the middle of the entrance with his bat in hand.

"I got our first name, little bat. Let's go shopping."

CHAPTER 15

ELIJAH

After taking Rain shopping, which shocked the shit out of her for whatever reason, I helped her get comfortable at home before leaving, alone, for Chapel. She is all set up watching some new documentary on The Night Stalker, she was so fucking excited. That guy was more fucked than I am, which is pretty impressive all in itself.

I let the fire from earlier burn itself out, it was nothing more than glowing embers by the time we got back and was used for nothing more than dramatics, just like that fucker does.

As I pull up to The Chapel, I see he has called everyone in as the field is full of parked cars. I park in front of the entrance and turn my car off. Before getting out I check my phone, pulling up the house's security system and I am satisfied seeing it is still armed.

Only a moron would try to get through it, it's state of the fucking art. The windows are made of bullet-proof glass and have a black tint when alarmed, so no one can see in but I can see out. Steel doors cover all access points in the house, including the garage. Cameras surround the area, and the front gate and perimeter fencing are electric. Living back home in Montana, this was normal at my dad's house, it kept us safe, so I made sure to install the same setup here.

Satisfied that everything is ok at home, I get out of my car and grab my supplies from the trunk. I am not one to wear the garb the rest wear, he knows not to push it on me either.

I put my mask over my tattooed face, it's a white rabbit mask covering my entire face. It looks so real and nothing like the cartoon ones. The ears are tall, standing past the top of my head. I did decorate it a bit with some dark dirt, it was too clean but now it's almost perfect. Only the addition of blood splatter would make it perfect.

The mask is something I picked out today while my little bat was shopping. I got her one too, but I haven't shown her yet. I grab my bat and close the trunk and head inside.

As I make my way through all the dimly lit tunnels

and passages, I swing my bat mindlessly in my hand. I don't run into another person until I hit the main room, that's where I find everyone. Stopping in the archway, I lean against the rock, crossing my foot over the other and observe.

Master, my stepfather, is at the front rambling on about some bullshit. Lying to his people about what happened at his third's house last night. I think the guy's name is Oliver or some shit, but no one goes by names here. He is known as the Master's third. His second and my mother are also standing up there, behind him.

"It was a terrible tragedy. His son was troubled. He tried to get him help, but none of it worked."

He is framing it as a murder-suicide. This fucker. I smirk under my mask, shaking my head.

Why am I not surprised?

"But The Dark One is giving him the strength he needs to get through it all. With that, The Dark One has also commanded us to gather here tonight, he has a name for the next La Notte del Diavolo in one week's time. Elijah, my boy. You have arrived just in time."

I don't acknowledge him. Instead, waiting for him to continue.

"Rain Mills."

The room remains quiet, and I am sure the bastard is smiling under that mask. Thinking he has won. Like

I didn't see this shit coming. Because I did. I saw this a fucking mile away.

It takes every bit of self-control not to shout Rain Sinclair back at him. Instead, I nod once before standing straight and turning to leave. I never stay for the entire meeting. Not wanting to show my hand and my fucking annoyance at his idiocy, I keep with that which I usually do and leave once I get the name.

His voice stops me. "The Dark One doesn't take kindly to disobedience. It would be best to keep that in mind."

I think you mean you don't, is what I think before walking away. I drag my bat behind me as I walk back the same way I came. Then, I hear my name echoing through the hall, "Elijah, hold on." I recognize the voice, but I continue walking. Footsteps race behind me. "He is doing this to get to you. Don't be stupid. Please, or The Dark One will call your name next."

I blow out a breath before shouting back, "Go back to your husband."

Pulling up to the house, I stop just before the gate and disarm the alarm. My mask and bat are next to me on the passenger seat. Looking at it, I think about all the fun we'll have together.

The gate opens, and I drive in, heading down the

long driveway and pulling up to the house to park outside. I grab my stuff and head in.

As I walk into the living room, I see the television is still on and Rain is leaning forward, entranced by The Night Stalker.

"Do I need to pause this, or are you going to come watch with me?" She asks.

Ignoring her question, I get straight to the point. "He gave me your name."

That is enough for her to hit pause. She moves quickly, turning to face me with a fuzzy blanket wrapped around her.

"What do we do?" She's worried, it's cute.

I walk up to her on the other side of the couch, holding my bat. Her eyes watch me as I lean in, her body pressing against the cushions. I drop my things to the ground and grab her face with both my hands.

"We get to them first, little bat."

A sinister smile spreads across her face, and her eyes gleam in delight.

That's my fucking girl.

She takes control, her lips smash against mine and her teeth nip, pulling at my lip ring. It stings, but I fucking love it.

My cock is already hard as it strains against my black pants. I pull back, but she bites onto my lip ring harder. I try to pull back again, but she keeps hold of it, one more move and it's being torn through my skin.

She seems impressed with herself, but she is only going to get herself in trouble if it gets that far.

Before I speak, she lets go and licks her own lips in satisfaction.

If she wants to play, we will play. "On your knees, crawl to me."

CHAPTER 16

RAIN

My nipples harden, and my pussy tingles at his command. I squeeze my thighs together as I am still kneeling on the couch, leaning over the back of it. Taking him in, he is absolutely stunning, butterflies flutter in my stomach as he arches his brow at me, as if to say, *don't make me say it again.*

My heart is racing as I push myself off the back of the couch. Turning around, I slowly move myself down. Lowering myself to the ground, wearing his black tee and just a pair of panties, I begin to crawl along the dark wooden floor. It's cool against my hands and knees, causing a chill to go up my spine. It is a mix of the cold floor, excitement and anticipation. What will he have me do once I get to him?

Crawling the length of the couch, I can feel his eyes

on me which brings me great satisfaction. Popping my booty out a tad, the shirt rides up slightly, exposing me more to him, teasing the teaser. I can play too.

Turning at the end, I slowly make my way over to him, looking up and keeping eye contact. It's hard not to, his eyes are captivating, the blue with brown specks, so uniquely him. He has long lashes framing them, which only adds to the allure, along with the dark shading around his eyes from his tattoo. His metal septum piercing glimmers in the dim lighting.

He is all fucking mine.

It remains unsaid, but I own him as much as he owns me.

Licking my lips, I am salivating at the thought. To have been captivated by someone so strongly, the urge to possess them takes over. To have ownership over their body and soul, and in return you give it back to them.

That is Elijah and I.

He acted upon it first, and I willfully followed. And I forever will, through the hottest flames and ends of the earth. Nothing can break us, and no bond will ever be stronger.

These all remain unspoken, never needing to be said because we know. One look is all it takes, our energy connects, and our minds speak. We understand it all. We feel it all.

I feel lust and devotion radiating off him as I

reach his boot-clad feet. He feels it back from me, irrevocably. We still have so much to learn about each other, to explore and I am so fucking excited. He has put fire and passion into my veins. Finally discovering who I am, no longer lost working at the local bar.

I am home.

Perhaps the stress of the past week has caused me to completely lose my mind and all senses of reality. If so, I don't want them back.

"Take my cock out." His eyes are hooded as he speaks.

Reaching up, my fingers are trembling in anticipation as I unlatch his belt, followed by undoing his pants button and slowly unzipping. My breathing is heavy as it lowers, and his cock strains against the fabric. My fingers brush against it, causing it to twitch under my touch.

Once the zipper is down, I reach back up, grabbing the waistband of his black jeans and pull them down his strong legs until they bunch at his feet. I do the same with his tight boxer briefs, his cock becomes freed, springing out of its confined space with his silver cock ring, begging me to play with it, to pull it with my teeth and tease E.

My mouth salivates with anticipation, and his piercing makes me want to lick him more. I am desperate for this man.

"Open your mouth," he instructs me, his tone slightly amused by my reaction.

Obeying, I open it and stick out my tongue, waiting for him to shove his throbbing cock into my mouth. Instead, he looks down at me, smirking then spitting into my mouth.

"Don't you fucking swallow it or close your mouth. Keep it there."

My head nods slightly, so he knows I understand.

He takes his cock into his hand, it's dripping in precum, and he rubs his head along my lips. The jewelry is cool against them, then he moves to my tongue. Just one taste and I am addicted, I need more.

I need to touch him, feel him in every way possible.

Then in one rapid movement, he thrusts it against the back of my throat. I gag at the initial intrusion, while trying to relax my throat.

"Suck."

Wrapping my lips around it, his spit still coating my tongue, I hollow my cheeks and suck. He isn't gentle. He is Elijah.

My eyes never leave his face. His nostrils flare, he is feral.

His hands grip the back of my head as he continues to thrust into my mouth. I'm choking on his cock now, and he pushes it deeper, cutting off my oxygen and making my eyes begin to water. My lungs are desperate for a tiny taste of air.

E moves faster, gripping the hair at the crown of my head harder. His voice is raspy. "Fucking take it, little bat."

I do.

I'm unable to swallow, as I continue to gag on his cock, drool is dripping down my chin.

He completely owns me.

"When I come, don't you fucking swallow it. Savor it."

My tongue brushes along the underside of his cock, helping in coaxing his orgasm out. I need to taste him.

Then, a deep moan leaves his mouth as his warm release begins to coat my throat. He inches himself out from deep within my throat.

His salty, thick come ignites the taste buds on my tongue. So fucking good. I do my best not to take it all in. My reflex is battling my mind. I feel some start to drip out of my mouth while I wait for permission to enjoy his sweet release. I am yearning for it.

He pulls out of me completely, gripping his cock tightly and rapidly works it to get every last drop out. Some spills on my cheek and nose. My own pussy is aching now. This is the hottest thing I have ever had happen to me. To be claimed. This is what it feels like.

He slows his movements as we keep eye contact. Then as he lets go of his heavy, semi-hard cock, he nods. Giving me the permission I need.

Closing my mouth, I slowly take it all in. Pushing my tongue against the roof of my mouth, never wanting the flavor of his release to leave. My mouth begins to fill with saliva, forcing me to start swallowing.

E reaches his hand out, and using his thumb, he wipes the come off of my face. Just as I think he is going to push it between my lips and have me suck it off, he shocks me.

He pushes it into his mouth instead.

Savoring his own release. In an instant, I could come. This is hotter than anything I have ever seen before.

I squeeze my thighs together, and my body pleads to have its own orgasm. I am desperate with need. He would have to be blind not to see my aching desire.

Licking my lips clean, I reach down and grab ahold of his underwear and jeans and begin pulling them up. I tuck him as I reach his cock. Then he takes my hands, gently removing them from his zipper. He finishes it himself before cupping my face with his strong hand. I nustle into it, closing my eyes in comfort.

His deep, husky voice breaks the silence. "Do you want to visit your mom?"

CHAPTER 17

RAIN

My mom.

She's here.

Not the thought I want to be having as my pussy throbs.

But it makes sense to why I can feel her so strongly.

Ever since I arrived. She's here.

We hadn't had much time between last night and today, with me being stuck inside my head and him being summoned by my father.

I nod at him. "Yes, please." I whisper in response. My brain is still struggling on how to react as it is being pulled in multiple directions.

He places both his hands out in front of me, and I grab hold of them as I bring myself up to stand.

"I will always take care of you." He promises.

My body tingles as warmth invades. I wrap both my arms around him and bring my body against his, holding him as tight as I can. Elijah holds me tight in return. I never want to leave his safe space and comfort.

His scent is divine—a mix of musk and vanilla.

"Thank you." Is all I can say, whispering into his chest.

His voice is compassionate but commanding. "Little bat, you best put some pants and shoes on then. I will meet you at the back door."

I don't let go. Needing to stay in the moment just a little longer. He doesn't force it to end either. Which surprises me, I wasn't sure how he would handle something so intimate as this. But he lets me take his strength and comfort.

Taking one last deep breath of him in, I look up and kiss the underside of his chin before letting him go. I immediately miss his body, and his warmth against mine.

My feet pad against the hard, cold floors as I race to our bedroom closet. Turning the light on, I grab one of Elijah's hoodies and sweats, which I have to roll at the waist a couple times so they aren't so long on me. Finding my black hightops, I slide my feet into them and race back to him. Finding him at the back door, the porch lights are on and illuminating the backyard. He also has a flashlight sticking out of his pocket.

He reaches his hand out to me, walking towards him. I place mine in his. Our fingers intertwine, and E rubs the pad of his thumb in circular motions on the top of my hand in comfort.

The action surprises me. Making me wonder, does he realize that he is soothing my worries and anxiety? Perhaps he doesn't, regardless it's working.

Opening the back door, he leads us outside. The night is cold, crisp against my exposed skin. We walk across the wooden deck and down the three stairs to the grass. Our feet crunch against the lush grass as we pass where Elijah has his new firepit setup. He grabs the flashlight out of his pocket and turns it on. Shining it in front of us, towards the thick row of trees lining his property.

There is one tree in particular that catches my eye. It's tall, with large overhanging branches and dark green leaves. It has to be hundreds of years old, the trunk is thick with some exposed roots around it.

That's when I noticed it.

The fresh, dark earth that is piled in front.

"I have ordered her a marker, it just takes time for the marble to be engraved."

Letting go of his hand, my legs move as quick as my mind. As I reach her, my mom, my legs give out. Collapsing on top of the freshly dug earth, which is her peaceful final resting place.

My focus is on her.

I don't hear E behind me, but the light continues to shine. He is giving me space, and private time to talk to her.

"Why did he take you from me? I wasn't ready. I still needed you." I whisper as tears run down my face. I don't wipe them away, instead I allow them to fall, and to feel. To accept the emotions I had been battling, suppressing these past couple days.

I have to accept this in order to start healing.

A cold breeze blows by, and the leaves rustle in the trees.

My sweet girl. I always knew this would be a risk, once I found out who he was—your father. I protected you the best I could. He found us. He plotted. He abuses his influence. But hasn't won. He will never win. That boy behind you will never let him. He kills for you. He lives for you.

Mom.

I will always be with you. I am always here. But it's time for you to spread those wings. Soar. Take back the power your father is trying to take from you. Elijah will be with you every step of the way.

I bring my hands to my face, leaning forward and I cry. I allow myself to finally mourn my mother and my old life. My body shakes as I sob. This is therapeutic, not sad, the need to let it all out is overwhelming. To release it all is freeing.

I'm unsure of how long I stayed like this. Eventually I feel Elijah, his presence is getting closer. I know he doesn't get why I am sad, but I know he doesn't like seeing me this way. He doesn't speak, he knows I don't need words of comfort or reassurance right now. This situation is what it is, words won't change it.

Revenge will.

"His next name for La Notte del Diavolo is mine, mom."

She needs to know.

"He's angry, so he named me. But Elijah, he will keep me safe. He said we will get them first."

Saying it out loud hits differently than hearing it said to you. You feel more in control of the situation when you say it.

"How was tonight, and will you tell me how The Chapel started? I need to know in order to understand everything happening." I ask, turning my head to face Elijah who is now next to me on the grass.

"The great Master Maxton Montgomery stood proud with his number two and my mom at his side. His number three, the one whose family we slaughtered last night, wasn't there. He convinced his followers that the son acted out a murder-suicide." He pauses, letting me take that in before continuing.

"Your father convinced them with his charismatic personality and charm that the Devil himself speaks to him, communicates his wishes through your father to ensure they are fulfilled, to better the world. And when you think about it, to better the world from Blackwood, it's the biggest load of shit, but people bought into it. Here, you either love God or bow down to the Devil. He started holding Chapel at his house, in the backyard, and used the fire as the communication vessel between him and The Dark One. Seeing is believing, people started to believe. Maxton saw this as a great money opportunity as well. He started charging people to attend and to have The Dark One help them. At first, followers would moan about their bosses or neighbors being dicks to them, and suddenly The Dark One, during Devil's Night which they call, La Notte del Diavolo, would have blackmail ready for them to use against those people. As more people started buying into it, your father's ego grew. That's when he renamed himself Master and moved to the caves with the cloaks and masks. He also started charging people to be members, or followers as they are referred to. As they moved up his ranks, they would get charged more to attend and to be close to the Master. Then one day, blackmail turned into bodies. Blood rituals to thank The Dark One, to give souls back to him in gratitude. Anyone who was in the way of The Chapel, their soul became enslaved to The Dark One for eternity. Then, your father started using the fire to get names to appease his own agenda, which led me to you and your mom."

"Why us?" It sounds pathetic as I ask it, but I need to know.

"He has known where you two have been for some time. When your names were pulled, he expressed giving your mom, the evil in the world, to The Dark One. Then I would keep you, he told his followers that you and I would be the next generation to take over The Chapel. His only blood born and his stepson. He convinced the followers that your mom was evil, she kept you from him all these years. Denied him of his rights. He sent me around prior to your birthday, he planned La Notte del Diavolo for that night. I snuck into your room when you were working late one night, grabbed some hair from your brush so he could get it tested. It was a match, he is your father. Then I took you both. Before La Notte del Diavolo began, he told the followers the plan for the evening, at the wish of The Dark One, which is why you were covered in her blood and markings after I killed her. Then shit changed. Your father went back on his word, he wanted you to himself, like the sick fucker he is. But no one questioned him, except for me. Questioning him only enrages him. Provokes his beast more. Something I fucking love to do. When *he* decided plans had changed, I was not going to lay down quietly and take it. He thinks he still has some control over me because of my mother. That has no relevance to me. You were always fucking mine. Are MINE!"

His passion is chilling. Beautiful and fucking hot.

"Then why pull my name now?" I question, trying to wrap my head around all this new information.

He blows out a sigh. "He is going to try and take you away from me again. He is either going to try and kill me instead at the next La Notte del Diavolo, or change plans again and keep you, trap you, make you his personal prisoner. And who the fuck knows, maybe still try and kill me. He knows I will never rest until I have you back."

Elijah's face hardens. He's not with me right now, he is off in a world where people are taking me. I place my hand on his face and whisper, "No one is going to take me. I am safe with you. I am yours. You would never let them have me. We would never let it happen. You are teaching me. I am becoming stronger, and my wings are finally opening. I am free. I am your little bat, as you are my protector."

His face leans into my touch with each word spoken.

I continue, "Thank you for bringing my mom to me, to our home."

Looking at me, his face is stunning in this light, the highlights and shadows from the flashlight accentuate his features, his tattoo, and his softness. Calming him down, his face in my palm shows a vulnerable side I had not seen before. Even if it's just for a moment, it's a nice glimpse further into his being.

As he comes back to me, his face hardens and his

breathing regulates before he speaks up, "We should get to bed. He may have pulled your name, but we also have names of our own."

My stomach flutters in excitement, similar to when E told me to crawl to him. I smile, and my eyes widen with my mind racing, wondering who our name is. Standing up, I look down at him with eagerness in my voice, "Well, what are you doing still down on the grass? Let's go."

CHAPTER 18

ELIJAH

At the kitchen table, I am leaning back in my chair wearing a pair of gray sweatpants, no shirt which shows off all my ink and drinking a hot cup of fresh coffee. I am always an early riser, up with the sun. I wish I wasn't, but this is one thing I cannot control. The morning sun is shining through the large windows that overlook the back of my property, where Rain's mom is. Last night was a trip. But I'm glad it's all out now. She knows exactly the situation she has been put into, and she isn't scared away. She is ready to run into it with me, beside me, and proving it the other night was the hottest thing I had ever seen.

Feeling her before hearing or seeing, Rain, my little bat is up. Taking another sip of my coffee, I wait for her to join me.

Entering the large space, her dark hair is up in a ponytail and wearing my black tee, which barely covers her ass. Walking to the coffee machine, she pours some into the mug I left for her. Looking at me, Rain takes her first sip, and her hazel eyes smile in delight.

"Do you need to sleep attached to me all night?" She grumbles, taking another drink.

What a stupid fucking question!

"Yes."

She doesn't respond, knowing her efforts would be useless. I am never letting her go.

Padding over to the table, she takes a seat, placing her mug down in front of her, while taking me in. I watch her eyes roam up my body, nipping on her lip as her breath hitches. Her eyes meet mine, catching her. She isn't embarrassed. Instead, she winks at me as I lean further back in my chair. Placing my hand over my cock, I grab it and wink back at her.

Rain laughs, it's captivating, something I could listen to all day.

Then she asks, "What keeps you here?" Which catches me off guard. What does she mean? Why am I here?

"I live here."

Shaking her head, "No, sorry that came out wrong. Why do you stay? Why do you put up with his lies and feed into it?"

I rake my hand through my thick hair. "There are things about me that I don't want to share yet. Things that I left behind for a reason, because they will come back soon. Oh, so very soon. But for now, I get to pretend it's not there. That I don't have those responsibilities. So I stay. Killing doesn't bother me. Hurting people isn't a big deal. Just another day. Being step daddy dearest's killing and torture machine keeps me close, in the know and it fills a part of me that needs this. The kill, the hurting. The satisfaction from it can be compared to an addict taking a hit of their favorite drug. It's also why I had the skull face tattooed on me. I am a ghost. I am death. This is me."

Her head nods. "Ok."

Her energy doesn't change after what I just said. She accepts it, and she accepts me. I had never doubted it, but it's reassuring to see her reaction. None of this has ever mattered to me before. But with her, it does.

We still have a couple days before we take out our name from the fire. I still haven't told her who, she also has not asked.

"He meets with your dad like clockwork on Thursdays, it goes well into the night. They discuss Chapel shit and whatever else. That is our window. We will wait until he gets home, then snatch him like I did with you. The garage is where we will do it."

"I'm ready. I can do this." She reassures me. Not wanting to let me down. That would never happen.

"I know you can."

Her new-found confidence is slowly coming out, and it gets my dick hard.

I lean forward, grabbing her mug and placing it next to mine, she looks at me like I just killed a baby. So this is what gets her upset?

Standing, I walk over to where she's sitting and look down at her, turning my head slightly as I continue to take her in.

"Does talking about murder turn you on?"

She shakes her head in defiance.

"If I were to touch your pussy right now, would it be dripping? Are you a liar, little bat?"

Her thighs clench.

"Liars get punished, not rewarded."

She looks at me with such confidence, her hazel eyes piercing through me. "Then punish me."

I use my foot to move her chair out, which takes her by surprise. Then, gripping her under her arms, I force her to stand then pull her tee off and throw it to the side. Her nipples are hard, and tiny goosebumps decorate her body. She isn't shy, she doesn't try to cover herself, only her panties remain.

"Bend over, hands on the table." I instruct, my face remains neutral, not showing that I am affected by her.

Obeying me, she does as I command. Turning to face the long, dark wooden table and bending at the hip, she places both her hands flat on the top. Rain looks over her shoulder, challenging me and daring me to continue.

Challenge fucking accepted little bat.

Behind her, I move the chair completely out of the way, and the force of my push knocks it over crashing to the floor. Not phased, I use my foot to kick her legs further apart. My hand moves under her ass, trailing along her panties until I reach her pussy. The fabric is soaked.

I knew it.

Liar.

I know she has been aching for a release since last night, when she was sucking my cock. In her sleep last night, she used my leg, rubbing herself on my thigh. But I moved my leg away from her, stopping her from achieving what she was dying to do, come.

This will be no different. I told her liars get punished.

I touch her clit through the fabric with my knuckle, circling it a couple times before pulling back. Rain moans in agony.

"Elijah. Please." She begs.

I pull the waistband of her panties down with my fingers, and they brush against her soft skin along the way. Lowering them to her knees, I take the palm of my hand and rub her ass cheeks.

"These would look even better with my handprint on them." Is all I say, before pulling back and spanking her. Her skin cracks and her back arches under my hand when I connect.

She moans in pain, but the smirk on her face says she likes it.

I raise my hand back and spank her again and again in rapid succession.

Her skin is bright red, except for the spot where my handprint glows white. It is fucking beautiful. My chest fills with pride.

"Are you going to lie again?" I growl at her as I spin her around and lean my body against hers.

Nipping at my lip, her teeth dig into it before letting it go. Rain smirks. "Will you punish me like that if I do?"

"Yes."

"Then yes, I will."

Brat.

I rub my knuckles up the curves of her hips and past her waist, making my way over to her nipples. I grip one with my thumb and forefinger and pinch it. Her pelvis bucks against mine, causing my cock to get even harder, straining against my sweatpants.

I pull on it before letting it go. "You like my pain? My pleasure? Such a good fucking girl."

I pause before continuing. Looking into her dilated eyes, I whisper against her lips, "You don't get to come today."

Then step back, leaving her with her panties down her legs and bare.

As I walk away and leave the kitchen, I can hear her mumbling under her breath. She will see that the wait is going to be fucking worth it.

My phone starts to ring in my pocket, ruining the mood completely once I see who it is.

My mother.

She calls, and I don't answer. It's the same song and dance each time. Why she doesn't give up is beyond me, but I don't really care.

If I were to guess, my mother is calling to warn me not to disobey The Dark One's wishes.

Shoving my phone back in my pants pocket, I don't fucking care. That woman is just as fucked as the rest of them.

ELIJAH

It's Thursday—well technically Friday now. It's been a few days since the kitchen. Even longer since I have let Rain come. And way too fucking long since I've had my cock inside her pussy.

When her punishment starts to turn into a punishment for me, it's gone too fucking far. I readjust my cock as I sit here in my seat.

We are parked outside number two's house, waiting for him to get home from his Chapel meeting. It's nearly one in the morning, he should be pulling up any time now. Rain is in all black, her long dark hair frames her face and her eyes are closed as she sleeps next to me. We have been here since eleven, with the lights off and our seats leaned back, no one should be able to tell that we are in here. The street has been quiet since we arrived.

Bright lights catch my attention. They move as they shine toward us.

He is home.

Waiting until they pass me, I raise my head slightly to look out my tinted window and watch him. His blinker goes on as he turns into his driveway. Rarely does he use the garage to park in.

Once parked, he turns his car off and gets out. As it locks, his car lights flash a couple times, followed by a loud double beep. He looks around, taking in the area. Someone is paranoid.

Step daddy dearest must have them on high alert.

This is the best part, making them feel safe before I attack. Just like number three. He thought he got away with testing me, thinking my promise was a bluff. He later found out he was wrong.

Number two is now inside his home, I sit my seat back up and wake up Rain.

"Little bat, it's time to fly." I whisper while gently shaking her leg. Her body turns, and tired moans escape her mouth. Stretching her arms above her head as she lets out a loud yawn.

"Are you sure it's a good idea for me to come inside for this part?" She asks with her voice still full of sleep.

I am just going to chloroform him, like I did with her and her mom. But if she is going to do this with me, she is going to learn it all.

"Yes." Is all I say in response.

I lean over her and open my glove box to grab the tiny bottle and a white cloth and pass them to Rain. Closing the glovebox back up, I lean back up and open my car door. "Let's go."

RAIN

Putting the supplies in my pocket, I follow Elijah's lead and get out of the car. Just like last time, we keep it casual to not arouse any suspicion. He reaches his hand out behind him and I grab a hold, letting him lead us to our point of entry.

"Isn't it too soon? He isn't even sleeping yet." I question, as the thought crosses my mind.

E doesn't respond. He told me not to question him. But I don't understand why we aren't waiting.

"Knock on the door. He will see it's you and open it. I'll be off to the side. That's how we will get in." After he explains the plan, he lets go of my hand and allows me to take the lead. I walk up the pathway leading to the front door. Elijah covers his face further with the baggy hood of his sweater.

Reaching the door, I knock on it once, twice then three times. My eyes skim over to E, who has his body pressed against the house next to the door.

I hear the lock click and the doorknob turn, he is going to open it. The anticipation is exhilarating. It's going to work.

The door slowly opens, and I can see his eyes peeking through the crack. "Rain, you shouldn't be here." He scolds me. I don't recognize him. Before I can respond, Elijah is already in motion, using his strength to force the door open and the man falls back from the force.

As we enter, the man is scurrying backwards on the ground scared. I follow E inside and close the door behind me.

"No point in running or crawling." Elijah tells him casually.

The older man, wearing dress pants and a knitted sweater doesn't listen, he continues to move backwards.

Elijah takes four large steps to reach him. Then taking his boot-clad foot, he steps on the man's fingers. A shriek of terror escapes his mouth. I roll my eyes, it can't hurt that bad.

I grab the supplies from my pocket, opening the cap and pouring the chloroform onto the cloth, and make my way over to the man's face.

"I'll step on the other one if you don't stop moving, you stupid fucker." Elijah snaps at him.

The man listens, and his body trembles. A whimper even leaves his mouth.

I move the damp cloth up to his face and smother him with it over his nose and mouth. I keep it over his face until his body goes limp and he falls backwards on his own.

This was easier than I thought it would be. I expected more of a struggle, oh well.

He had accepted that this was the beginning of his end.

CHAPTER 20

RAIN

After the man, 'number two' had passed out, I went and pulled the car around to the back of the house. Elijah dragged him through the dark backyard and with my help, we threw him in the trunk.

We are home now in the garage.

I have never been out here before, it's incredible. The floor is polished concrete, with drains throughout. The walls are lined with stainless cabinets, counter-tops and a sink. Bright fluorescent lights hung above us, with a metal chair in the middle of the space. A heavy partition has been pulled shut, closing the rest of the garage off to us, making this area seem like a smaller space within the home.

Once we arrived, we hauled number two out of the trunk where he was still passed out and placed him in the metal chair. His wrists are bound behind his back with a pair of handcuffs, and leather straps are latched around his ankles. I'm sure I could refer to him by his real name rather than number two, but his name doesn't matter to me. His placement in my father's cult does. He is number two. He enables him. He participates willingly. He has to fucking go.

"E, do we have to wait for him to wake up?" He is leaning against the countertop in the garage as I walk over to him, standing between his legs. His eyes linger on my face, from my lips to moving slowly up to my nose and then my eyes.

"Open the cabinet behind me. Grab the vegetable peeler hanging on the right side next to the meat tenderizer."

Standing on my toes, I reach next to him, my body rubs against his. Opening the door I grab the item right where he said it would be. It is stainless, just like everything else in here.

Then he whispers in my ear, "Take the scissors on the trolly next to him, cut his sweater down the middle, all the way so he is exposed. Then use *this* to wake him up, little bat."

I bit my lip, and I am giddy with excitement.

Before stepping back, I grind my pelvis against his. A game I can play as well. Last time, watching me, he couldn't stop himself from fucking me, in the blood of our victim. This is no different, I can feel his hard cock pushing against his pants. This shit turns him on, and I am feeling as desperate as he is.

He doesn't react.

Which only tortures me more.

Before stepping back, I nip his bottom lip and pull on it with my teeth. His decorated face remains neutral, letting me have my way with him.

I apply a little more pressure with my teeth, then let it go. He still doesn't move but his eyes are slightly hooded. Pride erupts inside of me. But I don't let him see it. I can play this game too. Instead, I turn around, brushing my ass against him then walk towards number two.

Placing the peeler on the trolly, I grab the pair of scissors. Pulling at the hem of his sweater, I begin cutting. As I reach the neckline, I do one more cut and the fabric parts in the middle, falling to each side exposing his somewhat hairy chest and stomach.

Tilting my head, I think about what I can do to wake him up with what I have been given. It takes me a moment, but I know exactly what needs to be done. Placing the scissors back down, I collect the peeler. I place one hand on his collarbone, pushing him up tall as he is hunched over. Then I place my other hand, with the peeler, just above his erect nipple. Applying pressure, I slowly move the blades down his chest. Blood starts to trickle as I continue, once I reach his nipple I apply more pressure, needing to make sure I get it all.

I force my peeler blades over his erect nipple and slice it clean off him. More blood begins to flow down his body. Looking up, his eyes are open slightly as his head sways from side to side.

It's working.

I do the same to the other side, still pushing him up, I slide the peeler down. This time I move faster, using one fluid moment to slice his second nipple off. Number two yells in agony, finally becoming aware of what is happening.

Elijah walks up beside me, reaching up with a ball gag, placing it in number two's mouth then wrapping it around his head and buckling it up.

"This should muffle some of it." E mumbles before gripping number two's chin between his thumb and forefinger, ink lining his fingers.

"You are our bitch now."

E steps back and grabs a couple cords with clamps and attaches them to the metal chair. I follow the cords with my eyes, from the chair to the trolly, then off into the wall. As I follow the cords, trying to figure out what they could be for, E is already making his way over to the wall which has a red switch on it.

Without any hesitation, he flips.

Number two begins vibrating on the chair. His muscles clench and I can hear cracking sounds. His dark pants now have a wet spot on them, he has pissed himself. More snapping and tiny noises fill the space but I can't figure out where they are coming from.

Number two's muscles are stiff from the electricity, causing his head to vibrate viciously with his eyes squeezed shut.

Blood continues to drip down his chest and I am now noticing some coming from the corners of his mouth. A few more moments pass before E turns the switch back off. He walks back over to me. "It was his teeth against the ball breaking. His muscles were spasming, causing him to clench down even harder, causing them to break. I assume he tried to use his tongue at some point to try and stop it, but the chipped edges would have cut it."

I don't respond. I am taking it in.

I am not scared. More curious, wanting to learn. To make Elijah proud.

To make myself proud.

"Little bat, can you unclip the cables for me? While I teach our guest a valuable lesson. You do not touch what does not belong to you."

Elijah's words come out seething. His focus is solely on number two. I kneel down and unclamp the cord from where they are in the metal chair. The ends are still warm to touch as I place them back on the trolly.

As I go to stand, Elijah steps forward, his fist swings back and then connects with number two's jaw.

"Are you fucking looking at her?"

The man tries to cough as more blood trickles out of his gagged mouth. His nose has also started to bleed.

E grips the back of the chair with his hands, his knuckles white as he boxes number two in, getting right in his face.

"You do not touch what does not belong to you. You do not look at what doesn't belong to you." His voice rasps with each word spoken as he continues, "You know why you are here. He tried to steal her from me. You were going to touch what is mine. You wrote your death certificate, I am only fulfilling it."

Chills move up my spine, my mind and body are devouring each word Elijah speaks.

"Little bat, can you pass me the sledgehammer? It's under the counter behind you." E stays in place, not moving back. You can feel the anger radiating off his body. As I approach the counter, I bend down and see the sledgehammer lying horizontally on a couple brackets against the wall.

Gripping the wooden handle in my hand, I try to lift it but it barely budges. Bringing my other hand to the hammer. I lift it with every ounce of energy I have. It lifts off and the weight of it almost makes me drop it. Regaining my grip on it, I stand up and walk it over to E. He holds one hand out, hearing me coming up from behind. His eyes were still focused on number two.

Placing it in his strong hand, he grips the handle and I step back. My pussy is dripping. This is the hottest thing I have ever seen and barely anything has happened yet.

Leaning against the counter, I watch my man work.

ELIJAH

He had the audacity to look at her. Here in our fucking home.

Red is all I see. My vision is tunneled and this mother fucker won't live through the night.

"We have a fire too. Your name was given to us." I tell him, expressionless.

His eyes widened. If he didn't think we were serious before, he does now. Which shame on him, he knows what I am capable of. What we are now capable of together. Should have never doubted this would be his fate after seeing me at his door tonight.

The idiot starts to cry, he is an absolute mess with a mixture of blood, snot and now tears running down his face. His piss soaked pants begin to invade my nose, fucking reaks like ammonia.

Fucking pig.

Letting go of the chair I step back, and my wrist begins to swing the sledgehammer, just like I would if it were my bat.

My eyes zone in on his knees.

I grip the handle now with my other hand, I need to use all my strength and with all my momentum, I raise it over my shoulder then slam it down onto his knee cap.

Muffled screams of pain and agony try to escape his mouth. As I connect, loud pops and cracks fill the air. If his leg wasn't strapped to the chair it would be as limp as his small cock.

Not satisfied with just one knee, I do the same to the other. There is nothing more satisfying than avenging my little bat. I drop the hammer to the ground, it goes down hard, the mallet head hits the cement first, then falls to the side where I leave it.

I walk towards Rain, who is now standing where I once was against the counter. Taking my hand, I brush her pussy slowly with my fingers, over her pants, "Do you like watching me hurt people? Do you like knowing within a blink of an eye I would kill for you? Does your pussy ache from knowing you are the only one who can control me?" Her breath hitches.

"Yes. And as I would kill for you." she whispers back. Her pupils are dilated, as I continue to tease her.

"This one is mine, little bat."

Turning back to face the fat fucker. As much as I want to play with my food, my woman's pussy needs me more right now.

My eyes shift around the room when I get an idea. Walking to the sink, I grab a plastic bucket from under the sink and begin to fill it with water. Once it gets half way, I turn the water off and carry it over to where he is still sitting, blubbering on like an idiot.

I begin pouring the water slowly, over his head.

It drips down his body, absorbing into his sweater and pants. Covering his face and the gag, which has metal bits on it.

Once I am satisfied with how wet he is, I bring the bucket back to the sink, then walk back towards the wall with my red switch.

"Little bat, can you clamp him please? I would say on his nipples, but those are gone."

She giggles at my joke. Walking over to him, she puts the clamps on the metal chair again. She wants to light him up. That's my fucking girl.

Once she is clearly back, I turn it on. My eyes are entranced. His body reacts as the water amplifies the current rushing through his body. The voltage is on the highest level.

A familiar smell begins to fill the room.

Smoke starts to come from his body.

I don't let up.

His body starts to convulse.

Both his eyes widen.

Two thousand volts are rushing through his body.

More smoke comes from his head.

His hair begins to singe. The smell is repulsing.

Not wanting to start a fire. I turn the electricity off.

Observing for a moment, his body is limp. He doesn't move, and his head sags.

He is gone.

Now, only one remains. His time will come.

CHAPTER 21
RAIN

After Elijah was finished playing with number two, we undid his metal cuffs, which left burn marks on his wrists and unbuckled the leather straps at his ankles. His deadweight forced his body off the chair and onto the hard cement floor. His head bounced off it, and the cracking sound of his skull echoed in the small space. I felt nothing that I should have. No remorse. Not ashamed. Only pride.

Blood was still dripping from his body and the ball gag was still in his mouth.

The smell of burning flesh lingered, as my eyes watered from the horrendous smell.

Without a word, Elijah walked over to another cabinet, grabbed a large roll of clear plastic and threw it to the ground. I walked over to it and began to roll it out in front of me. Making sure it was long enough to fit the body. Once it was, E was behind me cutting it free, then he began to roll number two onto it. As his body reached the edge of the large plastic sheet, E rolled the body with it, wrapping him up like a present without a bow.

I stood admiring his work, our work.

Blood is smeared and his feet stick out of the end.

E then grabbed the roll of packing tape and began taping it up so number two couldn' roll out.

"Little bat, open the garage door and open the trunk of my car." Elijah instructed with extreme focus on the task before him.

As I did what he asked, the garage opened and I walked over to his car parked outside on the driveway. Behind me, I heard grunts but never looked back to see.

As I opened the trunk, I heard heavy footsteps from behind me. Moving out of the way, I went to the passenger side and got in. Looking in the rearview mirror, I tried to watch what he was doing, but the open trunk obstructed my view. The car bounced when he threw the body in, then the trunk slammed shut, causing the car to shake once more before he got in.

We didn't speak.

He started the car, grabbed my hand and squeezed it tight, reassuring me everything was going to be ok.

Now we are pulling up to The Chapel, it's early

hours of the morning, and the night sky is still looming above us. The stars are shining bright, as we speed past the trees lining the backroad.

Elijah's comforting voice fills the void space, "If anyone catches us, jump in the driver's seat and leave me. I can handle them. But if you stay my attention will be divided, protecting you and saving us."

He's right.

My heart will break if it comes to that. Leaving him behind and driving off with him in my rearview mirror would fucking kill me. But it makes sense.

I turn my head to look at him, his eyes remain focused on the road, and shadows cross his face. This man is beautiful.

Nodding my head, my voice comes out as a whisper, "I understand."

E doesn't respond, his energy is screaming, I can feel it. He is worried about me. He doesn't need to say it, I feel it. Our connection was built on this foundation, feeling each other's energy and it has only gotten stronger in the past few days.

The car begins to slow, the headlights turn off, and we are almost there.

"How many people do you think will be there?" I question.

"It could be empty, there could be a couple or everyone, this time I don't know." His response is honest and blunt, Elijah.

We pull up to the field where the followers usually park for Chapel. We are relying on the light of the night sky to reveal any possible threats. Squinting I try to make out objects in the dark, but it's nearly impossible.

"We need the headlights, this is dangerous." I try to convince him, but fail. He doesn't listen.

A part of me knows he knows this place like the back of his hand, I need to trust his instincts as I am completely out of my depth here.

As he slams on the brakes, the tires slide along the gravel and the car slides in front of the entrance, which is slightly lit from the torches inside.

"If anyone comes, you fucking go."

That's all he says before getting out. The door stays open and he moves quickly, opening the trunk and lugging the body of number two out. My eyes remain glued to the entrance, and I watch the light for shadows or movement. My heart feels like it is in my throat, trying to escape my body. My feet tap repetitively against the floor mat as my thumb twitches against my lap.

Faintly around me, I hear the sound of plastic being torn, it's loud, and it could bring attention.

My jaw is tightly clenched. *Come on Elijah, let's go.* I try to encourage him telepathically.

I hear the plastic being crumpled up and footsteps

against the gravel, when my eyes notice two shadows on the inside of the entrance wall.

Fuck.

My eyes widen as I prepare to hop into the driver's seat. At the same time, the trunk slams shut and Elijah races back inside the car.

"Hurry." I rush him, panicked, we have to move.

The door slams shut, he puts the car in reverse and we floor it out of here.

The headlights remain off as we race to leave. We are only feet away when the two shadows become bodies, revealing themselves outside.

I don't know how he does it, but he does, turning his headlights on at the exact right moment. They shine on the two people in their cloaks, who have just discovered a dead number two, outside of the front entrance of The Chapel.

We have just declared war.

CHAPTER 22

ELIJAH

Rain fell asleep on the drive home.

She is exhausted, still getting accustomed to her new life. This life isn't for everyone, but she fits into it perfectly. And I cannot wait for her to see the mask I got her, to match mine. I am saving that for our final play time, her father, the devil.

One thing I have noticed is that my little bat hasn't seemed sad anymore which must be a good sign. Perhaps her mom being close helps.

That night when we went out to see her mom, afterwards her aura changed. The sadness washed away, or hasn't shown as much as it had previously.

I don't normally give a shit if someone is upset, ever. With her, all I wanted to do was make her feel better, but I didn't know how.

We have been sitting in the driveway for an hour, not wanting to wake her, instead watching her. Her chest rising with each shallow breath. Her face is peaceful.

Every so often her nose scrunches, like she has just smelled something horrible. I wonder what she's dreaming about.

A piece of hair falls on her face, and I reach with my finger to gently move it out of the way. It causes her to stir, while remaining in her slumber.

Moving my head against the headrest, never did I think this would happen. To care so much for another person. To need this person so desperately that I would do anything for them. And to have that given back in return. She is my beginning and end. Rain Sinclair is the other half that I never knew I wanted, but now I need. If she were to ever leave me, I would leave too. Life is nothing but a bore without her in it. No purpose if she isn't next to me.

My eyes wander to her once more before deciding it's time to go inside.

Getting out of the car, I walk around to her side and open the door gently and unbuckle her seatbelt. Slowly, I move my hands under her legs and behind her back, as my body gets closer her body leans towards me. Her scent of coconut and vanilla comforts and calms me.

Lifting her up from the seat, her arms wrap around

my neck as her face rests in the crook of my neck. Closing the door with my foot, I walk us to the front door, unlocking it with my keypad code and head in. The space is quiet as we enter, the sound of my boots is the only sound as I walk towards our bedroom.

Instead of placing her in bed, I continue to our bathroom. My oversized tub is against one wall. Still keeping hold of her, I bend slightly to plug the drain and turn on the taps.

"Little bat, we're home. Time to wake up," I whisper in her ear. Her body stirs, but her eyes remain closed.

One more I try to coax her out of her sleep. "Rain. Let's have a bath before bed."

Her breath is heavy against my skin, and her voice is groggy. "Ok, Elijah."

A yawn escapes her as her head moves off my shoulder. Rain's eyes flutter open, still full of sleep.

"Hi." She whispers with a smile. Her eyes penetrate mine.

Kissing her forehead. "Hi, sweet girl."

Placing her down on her feet, she stands and begins to take her shoes and clothes off. Her hair is cute and messy, still in a ponytail. I follow suit, removing mine. Before we get in, I get one of her pink bath bombs which she bought the other day from under the sink and add it to the water.

As it dissolves I step in first, the water is perfect.

Inching my way down with my back against the tub, Rain follows. Spreading my legs, my knees both bent, she moves to sit against me. Her skin on mine. Her head rests under my chin as the water continues to rise.

Before the tub can overflow, I reach with my foot to turn the taps off. The silence fills the air and the smell of roses invades our senses.

"I am so proud of you, Rain Sinclair. You did so good tonight." My lips rest on the top of her head as I speak.

She nestles closer to me, my arms wrap around her naked body as she responds, "Thank you."

We sit in silence for a while longer, enjoying each other's presence and living in the moment.

"I want you to paint my face. When it's my father's turn. He needs to see that we can never be split up, we are one in the same. Nothing can break us. Nothing can come between us."

Squeezing her tighter in my arms, my cock is hard against her back entrance, but she doesn't seem to mind. "Of course. Anything you want. It. Is. Yours."

We stayed in the water for twenty more minutes.

She gets out first, and water droplets slide down her body. She is absolutely stunning. As she steps out, I follow and grab a plush towel, wrapping it around her and kissing her delicately on the lips. Never have I been so soft and gentle with a person.

She has changed me, just as I have changed her.

Rain walks out of the bathroom as I dry myself off quickly.

As I enter the bedroom, she is already in one of my tees, I slide on a pair of boxer briefs and we both climb into bed.

Pulling her close to me, I wrap my arm and leg around her under the blankets.

As much as I want to fuck her until she is screaming my name, not tonight.

I feel her drift off to sleep in my arms, my eyes are heavy and follow.

Something alerts me. Forcing my eyes open.

It's the ringtone of the front gate coming from my phone. Rain is no longer in my arms, and I can faintly see that she is cuddled in the blankets now on her side of the bed.

Not wanting it to wake her, I reach for my phone and answer the gate.

The camera from the gate plays on my screen, it's him.

I don't say anything, instead waiting for him to speak.

"Open the fucking gate, you ungrateful piece of shit." He shouts into the speaker.

I roll my eyes, like I would fucking listen to him.

"You have one job. One fucking job. The Dark One is threatening to give your name next, Elijah!"

Here we go.

"Don't think for a second I would stop it either. You are going against your own. For what? For her? The daughter of a whore, a slut and fucking peasant?"

The longer I don't give him the reaction he is looking for, the more irate he becomes.

"She takes after who raised her. She isn't a virgin. She spreads her legs for any dick that gives her attention, including you."

My face is burning, my heart begins to race and my hand grips my phone so hard I hear a crack.

"I've felt her pussy. Did she tell you? I bet she hasn't. Her bare pink pussy. It was dripping as my hand cupped it."

The anger rushing through my veins creates enough pressure behind my eyes that they feel like they could burst at any moment.

He. Fucking. Touched. Her.

He touched what's mine.

"E, don't let him get to you." Rain softly whispers, while gently placing her hand on top of my heart, "He wants you to react. He is desperate. He knows he is next."

"You're just like your mom. A pussy."

Throwing the blankets off me, I toss my phone and storm to the front door, then outside in just my underwear.

"E. Don't do it. This is what he wants."

Rain scurries behind me.

I may not have a use for my own mom but he has crossed the fucking line by bringing up my little bat.

Rain catches up to me as I continue to walk down the long, dark driveway.

"Don't. Please don't. His time is coming." She continues to plead with me.

I stop. Looking up to the sky, shaking my head. She's right.

"Fuck." I shout into the night.

My little bat is right. I'm not thinking. All I am seeing is his severed head on the end of an iron stake attached to my gate.

Looking down at her, her legs and feet are bare. She looks so tiny in my tee. Wrapping my arms around her, my voice seethes, "He touched you."

"And I hated it. I wanted to cry, to crawl into myself and hide. But he would have thrived on it more. To see me broken would have given him what he wanted. He made me bathe, cleanse myself in front of everyone."

Taking in each word, a feeling in my chest forms, pure passion and devotion.

"You are the strongest person I know." My voice rasps as my lips move against her ear.

I can't bring myself to let go of her as I continue to speak, "He's all yours. I will deliver him to you. You are my fucking depraved goddess."

Rain steps back, smiling as her hand reaches for mine, our fingers intertwine. As I continue to watch her, her smile goes from soft to sinister. I find myself smirking back at her. What is my little bat thinking?

"But first, let's play with our prey." Her voice purrs.

Tilting my head, I am not sure where she is going with this, but I allow her to take the lead.

She leads us further down the driveway, but stops before he is able to see us. We know he is still there as his voice echoes into the night, taunting me, us.

Rain lets go of my hand and uses both of hers to reach for the hem of her shirt. Lifting it, she slowly moves it up her body, her pussy is bare, with nothing covering it. Her breasts are perky, her nipples are hard and begging for me to bite them. As it goes over her head, she tosses it to the ground.

I follow her lead, removing my underwear and allowing it to fall to my feet. My cock is hard, gripping it, I squeeze it a couple times tightly while playing with my piercing on my head, which is already leaking precum.

"I only drip for you." Her voice is soft and seductive, "I only crawl for you. I only submit to you."

Stepping forward I grab ahold of her leg with my hand and hike it around my hip. She holds onto my shoulders for balance as I thrust hard into her. Throwing her head backward, exposing her delicate neck, I brush my lips against it. Feeling the goose-bumps softly decorating her skin.

Licking my teeth with my tongue, I open my mouth and bite. Her voice moans into the night.

The taste of copper tickles my tongue as her warm blood drips into my mouth. I suck, needing more.

I am ravenous.

"Fuck." She pants as one of her hands grips my thick, dark hair.

My tongue licks her neck as my teeth are still deep in her skin. My chest is heaving and I thrust rapidly inside of her tight cunt.

Releasing her from my grip, I feel the warmth of her blood trickle down my chin. My hands grip her waist as her leg tightens around me.

"Scream my fucking name." I rasp.

Another moan escapes from her lips, "Use me E. Fucking use me. I am your fucktoy. Completely at your mercy."

As each word registers in my dazed head, it creates a more urgent frenzy. A need to fill her full with my come. To have me dripping out of her, slowly moving down her leg.

To own her.

My cock and my piercing rub against her sensitive walls, working her to her breaking point.

My hips continue to buck against hers.

Faintly, I hear her father shouting behind us, "The vermin and his whore."

"Focus on me. I am fucking yours, always." Her voice brings me back.

That last word does it. Come begins shooting out of my throbbing cock, coating her walls. Her leg begins to tremble around me.

"Fill me. Use me. Own me." She encourages as her pussy milks my cock, coating her with her own release.

"I've owned you since the first time I saw you." Panting as we continue fucking in the night, "The same night you took ownership of me and my dark, deranged soul."

Rain whimpers as our movements slow.

I can feel both our hearts rapidly beating against our chests. Our breathing is heavy, a mixture of blood and sweat glistens on her skin, shining under the night sky. Sticking my tongue out, I lick the same spot I bit. Savoring the salty copper flavor. Then moving to kiss her, forcing her to taste herself.

She devours me. Our tongues dance, fighting for dominance. Rain nips at my bottom lip. My hand grips her throat, squeezing it tight as I pull my cock out of her.

Her leg unwraps from my hip, but our mouths remain connected. Rain grinds her pelvis into mine, my hand still gripping her neck.

Kissing her once more, I pull back slightly, my lips brush against hers as I cup her pussy with my free hand. "Push it out."

Her eyes open, looking into mine. She obeys.

Our mixture of come drips out of her as I collect it.

Letting go of her neck, I grip her face with my thumb and brush it against her blushing cheek.

"Lick it."

I move back slightly, bringing my palm up to her mouth. Rain bites her lip then sticks her tongue out, lapping up our release. Her eye contact never breaks with each lick.

My face fills with pride.

"My good fucking girl, aren't you little bat?" I praise.

She nods her head, taking the last bit in. Licking her lips, she gets what remains on them as well.

Completely forgetting the fucker at my gate, this moment is ours.

Rain places her tiny hand against mine, which is still gripping her face. "Let's go to bed, baby."

Leaning forward, I kiss her nose and let go of her face. Wrapping my arm around her neck, she wraps hers around my bare waist. We leave our clothes and start our walk back to the house.

Think you can touch my fucking girl and get away with it, mother fucker?

Nah. I don't think so.

We are coming.

CHAPTER 23

RAIN

omorrow.

Tomorrow night, we rise. We destroy. We take back our lives. My life.

In a matter of two weeks, everything changed for me.

I went from being unsure of what to do with life to being kidnapped by a cult. My mom was killed right before me, then I was covered in her blood and held prisoner by the devil himself, my father, the leader of The Chapel. A father I didn't know until then. A father who wanted to take me as his bride.

Sick bastard.

Then Elijah came.

My stepbrother, my savior, my life.

He has freed me in more ways than I can ever thank him for.

I have always belonged to him. Our souls were always destined to meet.

He killed my mom. I can still see her lying on the table. Our eyes were speaking to each other, saying our goodbyes. He did it because he had to.

My mom has told me to forgive him. She does. Because it was to save me.

Elijah, someone who doesn't feel much, felt something that night and afterwards. He brought her back here to be buried, so I could always be close to her. Never without her.

Tears well in my eyes. I am exhausted emotionally and mentally at this point.

But it is almost fucking over.

Tomorrow, we kill the man behind it all. The man who has ruined plenty of lives. From blackmail to murder. All for his own sick agenda. To feel power, to have control and money. And for what?

To have a group of mindless followers worship him?

Does he really think he is doing the devil's work? Does he truly believe he is a vessel for The Dark One? Those may be questions we will never truly know the answers to.

The man is a narcissist.

But none of that matters. Because tomorrow it ends.

I'm sitting on the couch in the living room. The

television is on more for background noise than for watching. Looking out the large windows, it's daytime and Elijah has built another fire in the back.

Watching him is amusing, he is in his all-black long-sleeved henley, which is rolled up onto his fore-arms, black skinny jeans and combat boots. The sun is shining down on his dark black hair and tattooed skin. He is beautiful.

Once he seems content with what he has built, E runs up the deck stairs, walking towards the window and taps on it. His voice is muffled as he shouts, "Hey, come out here for a minute."

My face lights up. This man, my fucking man. He kills without batting an eye and still gets excited, just like a little kid.

I can see him, but he can't see me due to the tinting he has on the windows. When he went outside, I was in here lounging. I debated messing with him. Acting like I am not still here. But I can't. His excite-ment is precious.

Smiling, I get up. I am in a pair of baggy black sweats and a black tank crop top. My hair is down, wavy over my shoulders. I don't bother getting shoes as I head to the back door.

Opening it, Elijah greets me, wrapping his arms around me, picking me up and swinging me around. I hold on tightly around his neck, giggling.

"Baby, we have our final name." Excitement radiates from him.

As he puts me down, I kiss his cheek, "Go on then. Who is it?" I play along, humoring his game.

Grabbing my hand, he drags me behind him towards the fire. This has to be the biggest one yet, the flames dance before me and are easily ten feet tall.

"Do you hear it?" He says softly.

My eyes shift back and forth, "I think so."

"What do you hear?"

Letting go of his hand, I wrap my arms around his torso, he holds me close as I give him my guess, "Master?"

"Fucking right. But, there is one more still. Listen closely now, little bat."

My brows furrow, unsure of who else he could be referencing.

Looking down at me, I look up at him confused and curious. His expression is blank, I am unable to read him. Who is the other name?

"Listen closely. If you really focus, you can hear it whisper." A breeze blows past us, he smiles wide showing his perfect white teeth. His canines I picture having my blood dripping from, biting my lip, he speaks, "My mom."

I absorb what he has decided. Deep down, I knew this was coming. He has known his mom his entire life, moved here with her. Put up with a lot of shit for her, including my father.

This decision wasn't made lightly, I am sure.

Nodding my head against his chest, "Okay. And your mom."

I don't question him. I promised I never would when it came to this.

A calmness washes over me. I can also feel it over him as he leans into me more. The energy has changed as we continue to stand, watching the bright colors flicker before us. Hearing the cracks of the wood burning as the daylight shines upon us.

The feeling makes me feel content, perhaps? Maybe it is reassurance that in this moment, this is where I am supposed to be. What I am supposed to be doing. I don't feel scared. I am not second-guessing anything. My brain isn't riddling off *what if* scenarios.

But I do wonder, what happens after this?

"What's next? After tomorrow." I ask. He doesn't answer immediately.

We stand in our surroundings, as I wait for him to answer.

When he does, he lets out a sigh first, "We have one more day of living in the now. After tomorrow, what comes next, it will consume us. But now it is always going to be us, regardless of what is coming."

There is a part of his life that I have been curious about. But this isn't the first time he has asked for us to live in this moment and not worry about the future yet. I don't push it. He will tell me. Once this is over, I trust him.

Rubbing my hand against his stomach, "Okay. As long as it's always us, that's what matters."

Kissing the top of my head, he says with absolute certainty, "Never fucking doubt it."

ELIJAH

Holding Rain close, I never want to let her go. And I won't. She is always mine.

But I will have to tell her what's next. Time is ticking and it is not on our side. Eventually, I will get the call and we will have to go.

Before, it didn't bother me. Before Rain, nothing mattered to me. I was content and accepted what my future meant.

Now I don't want to think about it.

My phone vibrates in my pants pocket, Rain is still cuddled against me as I reach for it.

It's him. Her father. Maxton fucking Montgomery.

Answering, I put it on speaker so she can hear, I'm already short with him, "What?"

"Don't *what* me, boy. The shit you have pulled these last few nights is done. You bring her in tomorrow, or it will be you next. Do you fucking hear me?" He shouts, he is seething which makes me smile.

"She will be there. When haven't I brought a name for The Dark One?" I throw back at him. Rain and I talked after we fucked in the driveway. In order for him to not have his guard up at Devil's Night, we need to play his game and make him think he was winning

"Good. You better remember your place. Who you fucking answer to. I shouldn't have to call and remind you like this."

He is really laying it on thick.

"I understand. I needed to get some shit out of my system." Rolling my eyes while each word is a lie, leaving my lips.

"Don't think for a second I won't fuck her in front of you before I kill her. Remember that when you take her for the last time."

Then the call ends.

She squeezes me hard. Trying to comfort me, knowing how fucking crazy the thought of that makes me. My heart is pounding as images flash before me. Clenching my fists, my knuckles go white as I squeeze my eyes shut.

"E, you would never let him get that close to me." Her soft voice whispers to my demon.

"We have a plan. It will work. He will never win."

Her lips brush against my chin, "Come back to me, E. Come home."

My little bat knows me better than I do, always knowing what I need before I do.

"Please, E. I need you here. With me."

My heart rate starts to slow as my fists release and my teeth stop clenching. Breathing starts to return to normal, and my mind returns to my vision of the now instead of picturing his threats.

As my eyes flutter open, I look down to see hers, looking up at me with compassion.

Leaning down, I kiss her. Rain's soft lips against mine, it grounds me. As I pull back, she grips my face with her tiny hands and murmurs, "Welcome back, baby."

CHAPTER 24

RAIN

Getting ready for bed, I am in the bathroom brushing my teeth when I see E in the mirror, standing behind me. He's leaning against the wall, crossing his legs at his ankles and his hands go into his black sweatpants pockets. His chest is bare, decorated with intricate, beautiful ink designs. My eyes move down his arms and stop on the bat wings. I take in each line of each wing. Then, I look at mine through the mirror, examining them the same. A part of me still hates them and wants them covered.

But how he described me and the new meaning of little bat, spreading my wings and finally being free, finally being myself. Where I am supposed to be. They symbolize so much more than a fucking cult.

"You need to get out of your head."

Continuing to finish brushing my teeth. I don't respond, he's right. He knows it.

Placing my toothbrush in the holder, I turn around and face him, leaning against the counter. His eyes slowly linger on my body, just as mine did to him. From my bare legs to my oversized tee and up to my eyes. Slowly, he takes a step forward, his feet bare against the tile floor. His gaze doesn't falter from mine. As he reaches me, I can feel his breath on my skin as he looks down on me.

"Tomorrow. Once they see me, most of his followers will stand and watch. None are stupid enough to get between me and my target. I love the thrill, the pain and blood too much. They wouldn't stand a chance if they stepped up to defend him. It should be us and him. Should anyone try and stop us, I will handle it. If shit goes sideways, get out. Run the opposite way we came in. It will take you to the ocean. Caves line the coastline. Find one, get in it and stay there. I will find you."

I absorb what he is saying. I hate it, but nod in understanding.

"That is worse case, little bat. If everything goes how I think it will, your father will think I am bringing you to him. He will take the bait, you will kill him with the same dagger he had me kill your mother with. She will be with you as much as I will be. You have come so far, little bat. You are so fucking strong. Remember that tomorrow. Never doubt yourself." He pauses for a moment before continuing, "My mother is mine."

Grabbing onto his hands, I step into him, looking up, "Okay."

His mouth brushes against the crown of my head, my hair is in a pony, he lets go of my hands and grips it at the base. Yanking my hair down, my head is thrown back, and Elijah is right in my face now. "Nothing can happen to you tomorrow. Do you get that? Without you, there is no me."

I feel each of his words, they give me a small glimpse into the heart he has been so protective over. Chills rush up my spine, his face is stern and serious but his words express it all.

He is scared.

He is worried.

So am I.

We can only have these thoughts tonight. Because tomorrow, not an inch of doubt can be in our minds.

I won't be a liability for him.

"You have the dagger still?"

His voice rasps, "Of course. It's yours. To help keep her close no matter where we are."

As fucked up as it is. Which it is on so many levels, it would take years for a therapist to dissect, but I get what he is saying. This is his romantic gesture.

As I move to kiss him, he beats me by letting go of my hair and hoisting me effortlessly onto the bathroom counter. My legs spread as he steps into them, and his cock is rock hard through his sweatpants as he grinds against me, taunting me with what I need.

"You want this?" His voice is rough, and his mouth smirks.

My eyes look up at him, begging for him to give us the fucking we need. I don't want to be gentle with him. Not now. How he is with me, makes me feel alive for the first time in twenty-one years.

His finger begins to caress one of my nipples, circling it until it is nearly piercing through my top. My breathing picks up with each movement he makes on me. Biting my lip, I keep eye contact with him.

Moving his finger slowly up my chest, he brushes my collar bone, and then strokes my neck moving up my jaw. E pushes his finger between my lips. "Suck."

Using my tongue, I skim the underside of his finger, as I would if it were his massive cock in my mouth. The thought of his cock leaking into my mouth makes my mouth water.

Hollowing my cheeks, I begin sucking, moving my mouth ever so slightly back and forth, taking him as deep as I can. Using my teeth I graze his skin, his breath hitches and his eyes have now hooded.

Elijah grips my jaw with his other hand. He pulls his finger out of my mouth and smashes his lips against mine, devouring me. Our tongues lap each other, and our teeth scrape, clattering against one another. But it doesn't stop us.

He grips my hair again, pulling me back as we break apart, panting. His eyes examine me, moving across my face and down my body.

Completely at his mercy.

I reach up to touch his face, but he doesn't move or stop me. His eyes show he is curious.

My fingers trace along the beautiful black ink detail decorating his face, from the lines around his eyes, the shading it's filled with, to his nose which gives the illusion of being hollowed, and the lines coming from each side of his lips going to his cheeks. Then I touch his lips, lines run down them as well, "Mine. My beautiful man." My voice purrs.

Catching me off guard, his mouth opens and his teeth bite down gently on my fingers.

A part of me hopes he bites harder, to break my skin, to taste all of me. He can sense it as he releases my fingers and chuckles.

"This will be rough and fast. We take what we both fucking need. After tomorrow, we can spend days devouring one another. To do anything we fucking want. You will be begging me to stop by the end."

My head tilts, challenging him "Or you will be begging me."

E pulls my hair harder, and his mouth goes next to my ear, whispering, "Challenge accepted, little bat."

My pussy is throbbing, he is edging me with need as he begins to grind against me again. I feel his hand gripping my thigh, roughly moving up as his thumb circles my skin with each movement. As he reaches my hip, he slowly moves until his knuckles begin to skim down the hem of my panties. Slipping a finger underneath, he pulls the part covering my pussy to the side.

"I'm on my period."

My statement doesn't seem to bother him.

His fingers tease my swollen lips, then finding the string to my tampon, he pulls it out. Dropping it on the tiled floor.

"Take my cock out." He demands.

I grip the waistband of his pants and pull them down as far as I can, considering my current state, then reach down the front and pull his hard cock out. My hand grips it, then begins stroking it back and forth. Precum leaks from his tip as my thumb rubs it, teasing him.

"Let go. This is my show." His teeth are gritting, which means I am getting to him. I take this as a win, smiling back.

As I let go, he replaced my hand with his. Lining up his cock to my entrance, he slams into me. My back arches as my pelvis meets his, and a loud moan leaves my mouth.

We never break eye contact.

E wraps my hair around his fist, giving him a better grip on me. It stings at the crown of my head, but equally feels fucking incredible.

Wrapping my legs around him, my ankles meet, crossing over each other and locking in place. My hands are gripping the counter ledge for balance. E lets go of my panties, now gripping my hip under my sleep shirt. He pounds into me with more force each time. I know I am going to hurt tomorrow, hopefully bruise, so I am reminded each time I move.

Because this fucking man owns me.

My clit rubs against his pelvis as he grinds against me. His thick cock rubs against the walls at the same time. My body begins to tingle. Just as I think I am about to orgasm he stops, and a whimper leaves my mouth, I am aching.

Elijah pulls my hair harder as he resumes pounding into me. My pussy clamps around him as the familiar tingle comes back.

His voice rasps, "Come."

I do.

My entire body tingles and begins to shake as I come around his cock. It's taking everything I have to keep my eyes in contact with his. His movement becomes more rapid as I feel ropes of his warm come begin to coat me. My hands grip the counter, and my knuckles turn white as I continue to use him as my orgasm flows through me.

"My fucking good girl. Aren't you? Listening to me. Obeying me. Coming for me." He praises.

Nodding my head, my heart races as I respond, breathless, "Always."

Our movement starts to slow as we come down from the high. E releases my hair, placing one hand on either side of me.

My legs stay wrapped around him as our movements stop. We stay like this for a bit, neither of us wanting to move. His forehead rests against mine, we are both sticky from sweat.

"I am always keeping you." His voice rasps, confessing.

My eyes close, taking in his words.

He wants to keep me. My body wants to cry, but I won't allow it. Suppressing that feeling instead, as I continue to absorb the magnitude of what he has said. Spoken and not.

"Promise?"

His lips kiss the tip of my nose, then whispers, "Promise."

I nod, then grip his face with my tiny hands and open my eyes to look back at him, "Good. Because I am always keeping you."

He swallows, as if he is relieved by my response. He isn't used to being vulnerable.

Moving back, E pulls out of me, and my pussy drips with our release. It is mixed with my period blood, which is also dripping off his cock. Instead of pulling his pants up, he removes my legs from his hips and gingerly lets them go.

E then kicks his sweats free from around his ankles, and bending over he picks them up.

Bringing them up to my pussy, E begins to wipe me clean. Then he opens the cabinet, grabs something quickly and then closes it. He tears the plastic wrap off the new tampon, lines the applicator up to me and pushes the new tampon inside of me.

Once he is satisfied, E slides my panties back over my exposed area, throws his sweats in the hamper. Grabbing the used tampon from the floor, he disposes everything into the garbage bin.

Blood stains my thighs.

Jumping down from the counter, I noticed some left behind where I was sitting as well. Something I decide I'll clean in the morning.

His cock ring also catches my eye, which also has my blood glistening on it. It makes me feel possessive. This is how E must feel, but all the time with me.

I like it.

Walking out of the bathroom, I jump into our bed. He comes up next to me, taking my blankets and tucks me in tight, like a cocoon. E walks over to his side, getting in under the cover, rolls over to face me, and doesn't say another word, instead just watching me. His eyes seem different—proud, happy, lust or perhaps love? Regardless, I will take it all or whatever he is capable of giving me, because we are never going to be apart.

Tomorrow solidifies our bond.

TEXTS

Maxton: I do not recommend you
testing me, boy.

Maxton: The Dark One has called her
name. YOU will bring her to us!

> Elijah: I heard you the first fucking
> time. She will be there. Her pussy is
> getting boring anyway.

Maxton: I knew you would get bored
of her. Just like I got bored of her
mother after one time.

> Elijah: Don't care.

Maxton: Ignorant boy. You will not
disrespect me.

Maxton: You will show up tonight. Or
we will come and get her.

Elijah: Shut the fuck up. I told you, I'm
bringing her.

Elijah:

CHAPTER 25

ELIJAH

We have been restless all day. The anticipation and anxiety of this event has riddled our bodies and minds. Her dad has sent me a couple texts, reminding me of this evening, La Notte del Diavolo. I have reassured him a couple of times that she will be there. I even hinted at being done with her and that he was right about me getting bored with her the odd time I did text back. But also being aware that there is a fine line between playing him and showing our cards. If I lay it on too thick then he will know, the man isn't stupid. He is the leader of a fucking cult, he didn't get here based on his charisma alone.

Rain has been somber, internalizing it for the most part. Her eyes give it away—the anxiety. I haven't brought it up, instead letting her think she is hiding it better than she is.

The sun has been set for an hour. The clock is ticking, it's almost time to get ready.

"E, can you come help me?" Rain shouts from our room.

Getting up from the kitchen table, I walk through the house until I reach her.

As I walk into the bedroom, I look around but I can't see her. Walking towards the closet, she calls out again, "Bathroom."

Changing directions, my boot-clad feet take me to her.

The door is closed, which isn't usual for her when she is in here. I place my hand on the cold iron knob, turning it as I push it open. I am taken back by the sight before me.

Rain's hair is pulled back into a ponytail, and a black ribbon is wrapped around it and tied into a bow. She is wearing a white knee-length babydoll dress. It has a square neckline with ruffles on the shoulder straps. The belt is the same black ribbon as her hair, which is also tied into a bow. Her legs are bare, but her feet are clad in black flat Mary Jane-style shoes with white ruffled socks sticking out of them around her ankle.

My eyes move back up her delicate frame, which is adorned in the most beautiful dress. Her lips are colored with red lipstick, and her eyes have black winged liquid liner on them. Her lashes are full. As she looks up at me, my little bat screams innocence. But she is anything but that.

My breath is taken away. She is absolutely stunning.

"Do my face?" Her soft voice breaks my focus.

"Of course."

I lift her up onto the counter—the same one I fucked her on last night. My cock is hard and straining against my jeans. What I would do to fuck her right now. But I couldn't do that to her, she has spent several hours getting ready. She may decide to use the dagger to kill me instead if I do.

I reach over to the cabinet beside us, it's on the counter and reaches to the top of the mirrors. It's placed there to separate the two sinks. I grab my black eye pencil from it and take her face in once more. I know exactly what I am going to do.

Removing the cap, I warm up the pencil between my fingers by rubbing the tip. This makes it easier to apply on her skin.

Placing the tip over her forehead, "Keep completely still."

She whispers back, "I will."

Her warm breath tickles my face.

This moment might be the most intimate I have ever been a part of. It's more than sex. It's having a bond so close that you have the ultimate trust in one another. I can feel the energy radiating between us, we are the opposite ends of a magnet, pulling each other closer and closer. This girl has caused me to feel more in the little time I have known her than I have in my entire fucking life.

Pressing the liner to her skin, I begin. My eyes are focused on each line, and my hand remains steady with each stroke. Shading in just the right areas will add the effect I am looking for. With this, less is more. The pencil glides effortlessly along her skin.

With my other hand, I bring my thumb up to the area where I went darker, smudging it where I need more depth.

My head tilts as I carefully concentrate. A piece of hair falls over my forehead, raking my fingers through it. I brush it back.

Examining her face, I decide to add another detail running from her bottom lip to under her chin.

That finishing line completes it.

Placing the pencil liner down on the counter next to her, "Stay here. Don't look yet."

She nods, "I won't."

I wasn't sure when I would do this. But now it seems right.

Walking from the bathroom to our walk-in closet, I reach up to the top shelf, grabbing a polished dark wood box. The latch is made of gold, and it has her initials RS engraved on the top.

I'm not nervous as I walk back to her.

She is still where I left her as I walk in. Her legs are crossed at the ankle as she swings her feet. Her eyes look at me while also noticing the box in my hands. Her mouth smiles at my arrival.

I don't speak.

Placing the box on the counter, I lift the latch and slowly open it.

A small gasp leaves her mouth as she realizes what this is.

Grabbing it, I bring it up to her neck, the black leather looks beautiful against her. Rain remains still, but her breathing has quickened. Her eyes watch me the best they can. Placing it around her neck, I slide one end into the gold buckle of the collar. Making sure it's not too tight before doing it up, I slide a finger between the collar and her neck, the space is good so I continue.

"Can I see?" She speaks in a hushed tone.

Letting go of the collar, I help her down to her feet and take her in. She is wearing a part of me. Something I have never given to another before.

Brushing my fingers over the front of it, I kiss her on the top of her head, not wanting to ruin her makeup.

"Mine."

She grips my shirt as I say it.

My cock is still throbbing. Begging for her red lips to be wrapped around him.

Instead, I step back, placing my hands on her shoulders and gently spin her around.

She lets go of me, and her head tries to move quicker than her body so she can get a peek.

Once her eyes connect with her reflection in the mirror, a small gasp leaves her mouth as her fingers raise to touch the collar.

RAIN

I want to cry.

Not from sadness but from joy. My emotions are running rapid within me. Everything about what is staring back at me is precious.

"Elijah…"

He doesn't respond, instead he is watching me through the mirror taking it all in.

My face is perfectly decorated, minimal lines adorn it. A few areas are thicker and give the illusion of being chipped.

It makes me look like a broken porcelain doll. Stunning.

My eyes wander down to my neck.

My fingers are already rubbing against the soft, black leather. I can feel indentations. My fingers trace them, and I am able to make it out, On one side, I feel E&RS, and on the other LB. Smiling, I know exactly what they mean.

Elijah & Rain Sinclair and Little Bat.

In the middle, a piece is cut out. The area is lined with gold, and within the center is a clear glass vial with a gold lid. Within the glass vial, all you see is red.

A thin gold ring which has arms reaching out on either side wraps around the middle of the vial. This is what is holding it all in place.

My eyes meet his in the mirror.

"Thank you." Are the only words I can muster up. My eyes well with tears. I open them wider in hopes the air will stop them from running down my face.

"You're welcome, Rain Sinclair. My little bat."

CHAPTER 26

RAIN

My fingers haven't stopped touching the new addition around my neck since he put it on me. We are in the car, driving to The Chapel. He had me wait inside it while he loaded the trunk with everything we would need for this evening.

The road is dark, our headlights are the only thing lighting it.

My body feels calm since leaving the house. Something I did not anticipate.

Elijah's hand is resting on my thigh, every so often he gives it a hard squeeze, toying with me and my desperate need for his cock.

My body squirms out of discomfort as my panties are soaked. I tried to clench my thighs together earlier, but he slapped my leg in disapproval. The sting of it went right to my pussy, causing it to tingle with desire.

"I want to give you one too." My mouth spits out before my brain can stop it.

"What do you mean?"

"A vial of my blood to wear, to keep with you. I want to give you one too."

He nods. "Of course, little bat. Once this is over, we can do that."

A giggle escapes me from excitement. He laughs in return. It's deep, genuine and happy. I have never heard him do this before, it's refreshing. I hope he does a lot more of it moving forward.

We pull up to The Chapel, the opening where the followers park is clear with the exception of two cars.

"They aren't important. The main players should be here within the next thirty minutes, tops." Elijah reads my mind, explaining.

Instead of parking where he would normally, at the front he pulls his car closer to the treeline surrounding the area.

Once parked in the darkness, he turns the car off and looks to face me.

"Remember, run to the coast and hide if shit goes sideways. I will find you."

Worry tries to enter my mind, but I suppress it, pushing it way back, "Promise."

E reaches over me, smelling of musk. I take a deep

breath of him in as he opens his glovebox and reaches inside. Once he finds what he needs, he moves back, and I instantly miss his closeness. My eyes wander to his hand, and that's when I realize what he was reaching for.

The dagger.

He twirls it around his fingers effortlessly, then reaches it out to me.

Hesitating for only a moment, I reach out, gripping the cold metal handle.

"Good, now let's go have some fun, little bat."

CHAPTER 27
ELIJAH

My body still feels confused and slightly uncomfortable from the genuine laugh that just left my body. Showing feelings or emotions on that level outside of being in my element, taunting and playing with my prey, is still a foreign feeling to me. But I must have felt safe enough with her to let that happen so freely.

This only validates that what I feel for her is something beyond me, something rare and needs to be fucking protected.

We are out of the car now, and she has the dagger tucked under the black bow belt on her dress. As I open my trunk, a dim light comes on giving us some visual aid while grabbing the supplies. The first thing I take out is my bat, my trusted wooden bat. It has been with me through everything. I also have a couple supplies from my garage, if needed, a hammer, which I slide through my belt and my flamethrower.

My flamethrower is more compact than the ones with backpacks to hold the fuel—a mix of diesel and gasoline.

It has a smaller gas tank attached to the machine, once the gas is turned on all I need to do is light a flame, similar to how you would a barbeque, and she is ready to play with. I loop the strap over my head and under my arm, allowing it to hang off my back.

Lastly, I grab our rabbit masks.

I notice the corner of Rain's lips curve up. Her cracked porcelain doll face shadows perfectly under the night sky, lit by the moon and the stars.

Passing her one, she examines it before placing it over her face. The long ears look bigger with her short, petite frame. I dirtied it up, similar to mine so it isn't such a bright white.

It goes perfectly with what she has worn tonight.

My fucking depraved goddess.

I follow suit, sliding mine over my face.

Closing the trunk, I grab her soft hand into mine and lead us closer to where most people will park while keeping within the treeline.

"Those who see us and leave are smart. Those who see us and stay deserve this. If they don't see us, they should have been more aware of their surroundings." I explain under my breath to not make too much noise.

"Okay."

Her faith in me will never feel more real. But I will never take it for granted.

We stand and wait in silence, nothing more than the sounds of crickets filling the quiet space. As the first set of headlights approach, Rain yanks on my hand. I rub the top of her hand with my thumb, telling her I see them too.

She's excited, pulling her dagger out of her ribbon belt and holding it tightly in her other hand.

The lights don't shine on us as they pull up, it's when they turn the car to park that they do. The car stops briefly while the lights still shine on us, holding hands in our masks, our bat and dagger in hand.

Then the wheels spin rapidly against the earth, the car turns swiftly and takes off the same way it came.

They were smart.

More cars continue to come, and most of those who see us in the treeline drive off. Some stay, and others don't seem to notice us. More people have gone inside than left.

Aren't they in for a surprise.

The last two cars to arrive park directly up front, where I normally do. I know these are the last two once I recognize one of them. They completely avoid the treeline. As they get out you can hear them talking, it's her dad, the Chapel's Master. My mother and his number three.

As they walk through the entrance, which is lit by the fire torches further down, you can see they are wearing their black robes and white masks with the gold trim.

As they disappear down the long hallway, I lightly tug on Rain's hand to follow me. We get closer to the cars, and that's when I stop us. Turning to her, I hand over my bat, "Go stand by the entrance. I don't want you too close when I do this."

"Be safe about it, please Elijah."

Chuckling back to her, "I live for this shit, little bat. Don't worry."

Rain huffs out a deep breath as she walks away. Reaching around my back, I grip my flamethrower, swinging it over my head and positioning it under my arm. Turning on the gas first, I then get the lighter out of my front pants pocket. Flicking it on, I hold it up to light the flame and place the lighter back in my pocket.

"Jesus fucking Christ, Elijah." I hear Rain talk to herself.

Challenge accepted, little bat.

I don't plan on lighting them all on fire, just a select couple. We don't need the town noticing and drawing too much suspicion before we are done here.

I start with a car parked on the edge of the clearing, closer to the road. Pulling the trigger, I am standing a good ten feet away when the flame roars to life. Scorching the metals of the car, melting the tires once the heat pops them. The flames are hot against me. My face can also feel the heat of it through the mask.

It better not melt it.

Once I am satisfied, I move to another car, her dad's. I do the same thing, pulling the trigger and torching his tires as I walk around it. As I hit the windows, you can hear them break, the glass shatters as the inside ignites.

The beautiful smell of smoke and gas mixed together is intoxicating. But I must show restraint.

It's all about the long game.

Turning off the gas, the smaller flame goes out. I throw it back over my shoulder so it is resting on my back.

Walking over to Rain, she holds out my bat for me, I grip the neck of and take.

"Now it's time for the real party." I say while leaning into her, "Remember what I said."

As she nods her head, she speaks up quietly under her mask, "What was the point of that?"

Shaking my head, "It's a slow burn, you'll see. Plus, who doesn't want to use their flamethrower and cause an explosion or two?"

My answer seems logical to me. Little bat doesn't question it further.

I walk in first, and she follows. As we go down the long, torch-lit hallway, no one is around. Keeping my guard up, my eyes and ears are on high alert. But no one comes out.

Normally, they have at least one or two wandering the halls, just in case someone from town tries to pry where they shouldn't.

"Do you think someone who saw us warned them?" Rain whispers, grabbing the back of my shirt. Shaking my head, "No. They knew it was me standing there. They know what I am capable of. Perhaps your father has changed it up, trying to throw me off because of the other night? Testing me, to see if I am still trustworthy. Who knows?"

Anything is fucking possible with this fucker.

She keeps a hold of me tightly as we continue our descent to the main area where La Notte del Diavolo is held.

We approach the entrance, and I stop just before it. I can hear the echoing of voices from inside.

"Little bat, stay here. Let me play their game before we reveal ours."

She doesn't need to respond. I know she understands.

Letting go of me, she moves to have her back

facing the wall next to the archway. She looks at me, giving me a nod of reassurance.

With that, I make my grand entrance, standing into the opening, my body leans against the wall, my legs cross and I prop my bat up next to me. My stepfather is standing at the front, reciting some speech. Clearing my throat, I make my presence known.

"Isn't it rude to start without your guest of honor?"

CHAPTER 28

MASTER

"The Dark One has summoned us once again this month. He has gifted The Chapel with not one but two La Notte del Diavolo! Rain, our Principessa Oscura, is being returned to where she rightfully belongs. To The Dark One, to The Chapel, to me, your Master."

Standing before my followers, all lined up in rows wearing their Chapel robes and masks. The sight brings pride to my heart.

I do notice a few are missing. A few cowards that The Dark One will punish when the time is right.

The light from the fire torches flicker, casting shadows as the flame dances. Faintly, you can hear the crashing of the ocean waves outside. Taking a deep breath in, I continue, "Elijah may be blinded by her used pussy. We have allowed him to get his fix. There-fore, I can reassure you all that he would never go against us. The Dark One gave us her name. He will bring her in. It's his duty!"

Looking around the room, he still isn't here. My heart races with anger, and I can feel my blood pressure rising.

Stepping back, my number three and wife are standing behind me. My number two would be with us if it weren't for that little shit. He thinks he can fuck with me. He has no idea how far I am willing to go.

Walking towards the always lit fire, I hold my hands out against it. The heat warms my skin as I close my eyes and begin to hum. My followers join in on the hum, it is how we channel The Dark One. I concentrate on bringing his words to me, so I can interpret them and present them to the people.

Energy rises inside of me. He is here. My humming gets louder as his presence intensifies. Hands shake before me as I throw my head back. Remaining focused, I concentrate on what he is trying to say. Whispers and low hush sounds invade my head.

Then I see it. Flashing before my closed eyes.

Raising my head, I lower my hands and face the crowd.

"She will be saved tonight. The Dark One is rewarding us. Rain is mine."

Low murmurs can be heard amongst everyone as I make The Dark Ones orders heard. Before I can continue, I am interrupted by a familiar voice, "Isn't it rude to start without your guest of honor?"

She is here. Close by. It's time. She is mine.

CHAPTER 29
ELIJAH

"I knew you would bring her. Tired of her already?" My stepfather questions, and his voice reeks of *I told you so.*

If only this motherfucker knew what was still to come.

Keeping my tone neutral, "Yup. Got bored of her. I knocked her out before coming. She's here, leaning against the wall. Where do you want her?"

He clasps his hands together with excitement, "Bring her to the sacrifice table, boy."

Looking over at it, I nod. As I prop myself up from where I was leaning, his loud voice overtakes the room again, "And take that fucking rabbit mask off. You are being disrespectful towards The Dark One."

"I don't think I will."

Propping my bat over my shoulder, I turn around to walk out when his ego takes over, needing to get the last word. "What is that?"

Stopping in my tracks, I don't bother to turn and face him. I already know what he is referencing, "A fucking flamethrower. In case a torch goes out."

He knows it's a lie, but he isn't smart enough to put it together himself, so I'm not worried.

"Your snarky attitude will not be tolerated in The Chapel, do you understand me? Now bring her to me."

It takes every ounce of restraint not to end him now. To watch him bleed out on the ground before me, begging for his worthless life like the vermin he is. But I can't, he belongs to Rain.

Walking to the hall, her face is turned toward me.

"Did you hear everything?"

She nods.

"Then you know what I need from you? I need you to play dead for me while I carry you over to the table."

Her head nods again. I am not sure if it is from fear or wanting to remain quiet.

"The element of surprise will catch him off guard. We will use that to our advantage. I believe in you, little bat."

Not giving her a chance to respond, I wedge my bat under my arm and swoop her in my arms, bridal style. Her arms reach around my neck.

"Little bat, I need you to go limp for me. Can you do that?"

"Yes, sorry. I wasn't thinking." She frantically responds.

"It's ok, sweet girl."

Her head falls back over my arm, and then her arms follow. One hangs at her side while the other has fallen over her stomach.

In a hushed whisper, "Good girl. Just like that."

My breath becomes heavy, and the mask has little to no circulation, which helps make me realize that I need to calm down.

"Boy. What's taking so long?" A thunderous shout comes from behind me.

Rolling my eyes, I don't respond.

With Rain in my arms, I make my way back through the arch and into the room. His followers have parted, creating a clear path for us which leads to the infamous table. The table where I killed her mother and many others before. None of which mattered like she does.

Nobody speaks as I walk past them. My boots are crunching against the gravel with each step. My mother and number three have since moved from where they stood, to standing next to the table. Maxton is standing at the head.

The table is bare, no shackles or weapons are in

sight. My brows furrow under my mask. He did just as I anticipated. Playing right into the palm of my hand.

Orders have changed, I see.

Reaching the long, dark wooden table, I gently place her down. Her body is still limp, so once she's laid down, I adjust her arms to lay flat next to her and straighten her bare legs.

"I see you dressed her up like you too?"

His question is rhetorical. But that doesn't stop me, "Naturally."

"The dagger?"

"The one I used on her mom. Only fitting to use it on her as well."

"Good job. The Dark One will reward you for this." His voice promises, even though I know it's false.

Not moving from her side, I await his next move.

Lowering my bat from under my arm, I grip it tightly in my hand, ready to use.

He turns to face her, raising his hands to her mask. Gripping it at the bottom, he slowly removes it from her face, sliding it up until the strap under her head is freed.

Her eyes are closed, lashes resting on her face as her breath is slow but even. The face cracks are still perfectly in place—my little broken doll, my little bat. So beautiful laying before me.

Her father drops the white rabbit mask to the ground, the plastic makes the crinkling sound as it hits the ground. And for the first time, he sees her for who she is.

Mine.

"Is this your idea of being funny? Bringing her to me, your Master and The Dark One, dressed like this. Wearing this face paint with a fucking collar around her neck? She isn't your fucking doll, boy."

Curt in my response, "Am I laughing?"

"You were always fucking sick in the head. This, this is next fucking level from you, boy. To come here, embarrass me, the members of The Chapel like this. You should be fucking ashamed of yourself. And your mother will be punished for your insubordinate behavior."

He threatens me, by using my mother, like it would have an effect on me.

No emotion comes to light with his words.

No panic or pleading for mercy.

My life only holds value for her, Rain.

Unamused by his antics, I step towards him, openly challenging him. A few gasps can be heard from behind me, but I pay them no attention. This isn't for them. They are as filthy as he is.

"Can we get on with it, already?"

Clearing his throat, again with the fucking old man dramatics, "The Dark One spoke to us before you graced us with your presence. He has saved her. After enabling us with two La Notte del Diavolo this month, he has also gifted us with saving our Principessa Oscura. She will be mine by the end of the night."

I don't move.

He is waiting for it. Banking on it. But I let him carry on.

"In her place, The Dark One has requested your mother."

Of course he did.

A gasp can be heard, my mother.

Smirking under my mask, this is fucking perfect. She was mine anyway. He hasn't a fucking clue how perfectly this is going for me.

"Boy, wake her up. We have a ceremony and a sacrifice to perform." His arms rise in the air as he elevates his voice with each word. His followers clap in unison. None of them try to stop this, which only solidifies my plan for later.

Looking toward my mother, she stands there, all shock is washed away as she accepts her fate.

No fighting, no pleading.

We are so similar but also extremely different.

I am not stupid, she is.

Believing The Dark One is fucking real.

Pathetic.

"It is a great honor to be summoned by The Dark One like this." She says proudly.

Maxton's head snaps towards her. "Did anyone say you could speak, woman?"

Bowing her head, my mother submits to him.

"Elijah, wake her up. And remove that collar from around her neck. She will no longer be needing it." He instructs.

Turning my body towards Rain, I lower my head over hers, tilting my head slightly, taking her in one last time before absolute chaos ensues.

I whisper softly, so only she can hear, "Wait for my signal."

Her eyes are still closed, but she squints them ever so slightly, telling me she understands.

My mother is still standing off to the side, my stepfather has made his way over to her, they are speaking softly to each other, distracted.

His number three remains in place, standing closest to me.

Still bent over, I rotate my head to look at him. My free hand goes to my hip, where my hammer is hanging from my belt.

It's hard to tell if he has noticed or if he is too focused on my mask and my eyes staring at him. Standing up straight, I close the distance between him and me, pulling the hammer out of my belt. As I pull it up by its steelhead, I slide my hand down the wooden handle. Gripping it tightly, I then use all my momentum, swinging it directly where my eyes are aiming—the side of his thick skull.

Everything moves in slow motion.

My hammer is already propelling towards him before he even notices what is occurring.

As it connects with the side of his head before dropping to the ground. His mouth opens, yelling in pain as his body falls to the ground from the force of the impact.

Time speeds up, and I step over his body which is tossing around below. The hood of his robe has fallen off, while his mask remains. Loud wails of pain leave his mouth. Bending at the waist, I grip my hammer and continue my assault on him.

My movements are rapid, and each time I connect with his head, I come back for more. One after another, I am hyper-focused on this piece of shit. Blood splatters off him, flying up at me and around us each time I strike him. His head bounces against the ground, he is no longer in control. A pool of blood slowly starts to form around his head as well. Pieces of brain matter are getting stuck to the hammer now. My breathing is heavy. Staying bent over and staring at his lifeless body below me, I drop the hammer next to me.

Lifting my foot, I need to make sure he is gone, dead, with no chance of coming back. Where I have bashed his skull in, I place the heel of my boot and step down on him. His skull continues to break, as I feel his head moving down from the pressure I step back, removing my foot from his head. His head is angled up, still laying lifeless before me. I swing my foot and kick his jaw just under his chin. This causes his precious Chapel mask to come flying off. Beneath it, you can see one of his eyes has popped out, blood is coming out of his mouth and nose, and the force of the kick has caused him to bite his tongue off.

"Fuck you, motherfucker. Who's next?"

CHAPTER 30
RAIN

The sound of something hitting the ground can be heard next to me, where I have been laying. I take that as the signal E was talking about.

With my mask now gone, they will notice as soon as I open my eyes.

So I have to move quickly.

As I open them, they take a moment to adjust to the dim lighting. Reaching my hand to my waist, I grab the dagger which is still tucked under my belt. As I wrap my fingers around the cold metal, my heart starts to race, but I cannot panic, it will only jeopardize us and make everything leading up to this moment a waste.

As I sit up and take in my surroundings, E is next to

me, obliterating whomever is on the ground with a hammer. Next to them stands my father and his mom.

Not noticing me, my father goes to move. Before he can, I hold up my arm with the dagger gripped tightly in my hand. One move, and I could have it impaled into his throat. My eyes stare at him, daring him to try me. To see if I am bluffing.

He would learn quickly that I am not.

"If anyone leaves this room, we will find you. We will burn you fucking alive. Do you understand me?" I shout, projecting my voice the loudest that I can go so everyone behind me doesn't miss a word I have said.

From the corner of my eye, I see E standing over a body. His chest is heaving, all I can see is blood. It's on the ground and splattered all over him.

"Fuck you, motherfucker. Who's next?"

His voice is full of hate, disgust and rage.

This is another level of him that I have not seen, but need more. It's fucking spectacular. Elijah Sinclair is in his element. No one is getting out of here alive.

He doesn't look at me.

His gaze focuses on his mom and stepfather. Raising his hand, he points his finger at them, "You. I never thought you would sink to his level."

My own hand starts shaking as the adrenaline kicks in. A few footsteps can be heard behind me.

"She said no one fucking leaves. Are you deaf or

just stupid?" Elijah shouts into space. The footsteps immediately stop.

Gripping his bat tighter, he swings it around while his other hand goes to his mask. Removing it off his face, he throws it next to where mine lays. His focus never leaves the two standing in front of him.

As his face is revealed, his nostrils are flaring and the biggest grin adorns his face. His perfectly white, straight sharp teeth are showing.

Something so terrifying to most is breathtaking to me.

"Rain, you can put your hand down. If the narcissist tries anything, he knows he will end up like his friend here."

Listening to his direction, I lower the blade. Still sitting on the table, I move to the edge and jump off. Touching my collar, the vial and the engraved letters gives me the strength I need as I walk towards Elijah.

He never stops swinging his bat, and I think a part of it keeps him focused. Not doing anything, just standing still in a situation like this would drive him mental.

Passing him, he grabs my free hand with his. Bringing it to his mouth, Elijah kisses it softly. "You did so good, baby."

A smile forms on my face, and it's full of pride, "Thank you."

Releasing me gently, I go to take my place behind him but E stops me.

"Next to me, little bat."

Stopping in place, I turn around and stand next to him.

"You two are more stupid than I thought. The Dark One will punish you until your last breath for this. You will never escape him, or us. Don't you see that? What you are doing here is a waste." My father shouts.

Elijah's mouth closes, his smile is gone.

"I highly doubt that." E's tone makes him sound bored. Then a wad of spit flies out of his mouth, landing directly on my father's white mask, just above his eye.

Just as I am about to wish it had landed on his eye, it drips slowly from the rim of the eye hole onto his lashes. This brings a smile of satisfaction to my face. As for my father, he is pissed. His mask goes flying off as he uses the sleeve of his robe to wipe his face.

This is the first time I have seen his face.

I've not asked for a picture in all this time. It never crossed my mind.

His brows are dark and bushy, and a chiseled jawline with thin lips. Tanned skin and brown eyes. His nose is long and pointy, fitting.

"Get out of your head. You are nothing like him." E whispers, the tip of his finger brushes against my hand.

He's right. I know that. But it's like seeing anything for the first time, I'm just taking it in and absorbing it all.

My father steps forward, and before he can get too close, Elijah is on him. His bat is in the air and connects with the side of his head. You can hear the crack from the impact as my father stumbles to the ground, tripping as he goes down. The front of his head connects with the hard wooden table next to us. Bouncing him backwards as he falls to the ground, knocked out cold.

A feminine gasp moves my attention back up.

"He wouldn't have protected you anyways mother. The theatrics really aren't necessary. He isn't dead."

Elijah steps over my father's unconscious body, kicking dirt up as he does.

Looking towards The Chapel's followers, they are all still here. Some are holding hands, and some have their hands raised over their faces. A couple have fainted and are laying on the ground. They have stood by it all, and they will continue until this ends tonight.

Looking back towards E and his mom, he is now towering over her. He has at least a foot on her.

I stay in place, his mother is his.

CHAPTER 31
ELIJAH

This bitch.

This bitch thought she could get away with it. Thought that the mask protected her. That I would never find out.

Pathetic.

I'm ashamed to even call her my mother. I knew she was fucked by the fact that she left my dad for this sack of shit. But knowing what she did to Rain only solidifies it.

Whimpers come from behind her mask. She is scared. Or she thinks I give a fuck that she is sad.

I couldn't care less.

Wrapping my fingers around the side of her white mask, I pull it towards me with force, the thin ties break and it snaps off her face.

Her eyes are red, puffy and swollen from crying. Her lip trembles as she looks up at me.

"Your voice that day gave you away."

Her head shakes, and her face is confused. "What are you talking about?"

Playing stupid doesn't get you points with me.

Pointing towards the opening, I lower my mouth closer to her ear so she can really listen to the words coming out of my mouth, "Chasing us down the hall that day. Pleading with me. That's what gave you away."

Moving my head back and watching while she puts the pieces together.

Her eyes squint as they shift back and forth as she thinks back.

Then I see the exact moment she remembers.

Realization washes over her face. Eyes widen as her jaw drops, covering her mouth with her hands as she gasps theatrically.

"You hand fucking delivered her to him on a silver fucking platter."

My mom's head starts to shake back and forth as tears well in her eyes.

"I didn't know. Whatever he did, I didn't know." Her words are mumbled.

Liar.

"You stayed while he did it. You knew exactly what he did, you watched it happen and did nothing." My voice is seething, and each word is spoken through gritted teeth.

Reaching out, she touches my chest. "The Dark One, he tells us what is needed. We just follow his orders. Elijah. We don't have control over it."

Fucking delusional.

"I knew you were dumb. You left something good for this shit. But I didn't realize you were really this stupid."

Her face squints at me in confusion.

"Cut the shit, mom. For once in your life, use your goddamn brain and think."

She's starting to aggravate me, I'm not sure how much longer I can put up with it, honestly.

Her words come out with confidence, "He is the vessel, baby boy. The Dark One uses the Master as his voice."

Blowing out a deep breath, I look up to the ceiling.

She had her fucking chance, and I gave it to her. To come clean before it all ended.

I wouldn't describe this feeling coming over me as disappointment, I would have to care to feel that. Perhaps, I am just tired of the mindless bullshit.

That's what The Chapel is.

A bunch of mindless fuckers following a charismatic narcissist. I played along, and I got my fix of blood and torture. None of these people mattered to me. Not until her.

Nobody fucks with what is mine.

Looking back down at my mom, I can see she truly believes the bullshit spewing from her mouth. Her eyes plead with me to believe her too.

Not today.

Dropping my bat, it bounces to the ground next to me.

Digging into my pants pocket, I pull out my black switch blade. Clicking the side of the handle brings the sharp, shiny silver blade out.

"Fighting it will only make it worse." I promise her as I grab her arm.

She tries to pull it back but my grip is tight.

"Rain, roll up her sleeve."

Tiny footsteps start behind me.

Coming up beside me, her hand grips my mom's arm just above my hand as she pushes the robe's sleeve up.

Looking up at my mom, Rain reiterates what I have already promised, "The Dark One can't wait to meet you."

Audible gasps fill the room.

These dumb fucks believe my little bat is being serious Fuck me.

A few whisper, "She really is our dark princess, Principessa Oscura"

Being absolutely over this shit, I place the blade on my mom's skin just above her bat wings tattoo.

"No, please don't. My sweet baby boy, don't do this to your mother."

Begging will get you nowhere, or has she forgotten?

The countless lives that have begged in this same spot, each La Notte del Diavolo, have never convinced me to change my mind.

Digging the blade into the skin, I begin slicing her tattoo off, moving the sharp blade under her skin. Blood trickles down her arm, she is screaming in agony. Trying to move her arm, Rain keeps my mom's sleeve rolled up but also grips her arm at the elbow to stop her from moving as much.

Leaving Rain to hold her arm, I let go and grab the skin as it begins to hang off her. Then, in one rapid movement, I pull on it, ripping it down her arm the rest of the way.

A blood curdling scream fills my ears. Smiling, I'm glad she's hurting.

Her other hand fists, at first I think she is going to take a swing at me, but she doesn't. Moving it to her mouth, she bites down on it, her knuckles are white and her breathing is heavy.

Using the blade again, I make the final cut and the thick piece of skin falls to the ground. Blood is now flowing down her arm, building up where Rain's hand is holding her. Blood runs off and drips at our feet.

Mom has tears running down her face, snot

hanging from her nose and strings of saliva coming from her mouth.

"Thank you, little bat." I look at her, so fucking beautiful and kiss the top of her head.

Rain lets go of my mom, stepping back to stand next to me.

"The motherfucker on the ground should be up soon. It's time for you to go." My head tilts as her emotions change again, back to fear.

This is what gets me off.

People have many faces, you see their true one just before they die.

Nothing left to hide behind. Only unfiltered, raw emotion remains. Regret and fear—promises to change usually come next from those who are guilty of something.

Pure terror, worry and confusion come from those who are innocent.

I've seen it all.

Grabbing the strap of my flamethrower, I toss it over my shoulder, taking it off and holding it in front of me.

Taking the lighter from my pocket, I turn the gas on and light the flame then put the lighter back in my pocket.

Pointing it at my mom, her eyes widen and she immediately sobers.

"No, no, no. Don't do this. Please. My sweet baby boy, please." Her words stutter as she speaks.

Taking a step back, she thinks that will help. But I take a step forward.

Her robe sleeve has slid back down, and blood continues to flow down her hand.

"Keep moving backwards."

Nodding, she obeys.

Too bad for her, I am already steps ahead of her in this.

For each step back, I take one forward with my flamethrower aimed at her.

As we get closer, you can hear the crackle of the flames. Feel the heat radiating off the large fire.

Her head shakes, no. Mine nods, yes.

"Keep moving."

Her next step back is small—too small.

"It's going to happen. Those bitch steps will only make it take longer." The sooner she realizes I'm not going to push her in, the easier this will be.

She is going to walk into the fire herself.

"I can't." Her voice is faint.

Rolling my eyes, "You can. You fucking will. Rain didn't have a choice the day it was decided she would be cleansed. The day he fucking *touched* her while you stood by and watched with the rest of them. So just like her, your choices are gone too. Keep. Fucking. Walking."

My patience for this is wearing thin.

Placing the top of my thrower on her forehead, the tiny flame just below flickers. One pull of the trigger—that's all it would take.

Her teeth chatter as she steps back once more. Her back arches from the intense heat.

"Again, make it count."

Closing her eyes, mom begins whispering something to herself. It's too hushed for me to hear but I can see her lips moving. Applying pressure to the thrower still on her forehead, she takes another step.

The robe must be made of cheap fabric as the moment the flame touches it, it's engulfed.

Screams leave her mouth—short, loud screams.

Nudging her once more, she loses her footing and stumbles further back. Tripping over the rocks surrounding the fire, keeping it contained, mom falls backwards into the bright orange and red flames. Her arms reach out, her last bit of hope wasted. No one is reaching out to save you.

Putting the flame out on my thrower, I loop the strap back over and have it rest against my back, as I continue watching the sight before me.

My mom's feet are sticking out from where she tripped. Loud, ear-piercing screams fill the area. The followers, shocked, join in with panic.

Hearing a set of footsteps coming up behind me rapidly, I step out of the way. It's a brave moron, who must have thought they would push me in next. They are wrong.

As I move, they are running too quickly to stop. I use their own momentum against them, reaching out and pushing them in to join her.

Looking out at the room, I ask them again, "Who's next motherfucker?"

No one else steps up or responds, they stop reacting to the scene before us. One in the front has a wet spot around them, the bastard has pissed himself.

"That's what I thought."

Turning back towards the flame, the screams from within continue. Every so often, you can see an arm reaching inside of it. The smell of burnt flesh begins to overtake the room. If you haven't smelled it before, it's fucking terrible. Have you ever smelled burning hair? It's like that, but amplified.

I have blowtorched and electrocuted my fair share of people so it doesn't bother me anymore. But for beginners, like my little bat, this shit is not pleasant.

Something brushes against me, looking over it's Rain. I was so entranced by it all that I didn't even hear her coming up behind me.

Her fingers entwine in mine. The flame looks stunning, bouncing off her skin.

Then again, she always looks beautiful.

The screams begin to stop.

Burning alive is the most painful way to go. She got what she deserved.

As the room goes quiet, the cracking of the flame and wood takes over.

Turning us around, Rain takes the lead. We walk back towards her father, who is still lying on the ground. He is either still passed out or faking it in hopes we will forget about him.

Standing next to him, our hands are still connected as we both look down at him.

Rain lets out a sigh of frustration before kicking him in the ribs. The move surprises me, causing me to chuckle.

His head rolls left to right on the ground as an achy moan escapes his mouth.

Taunting him, Rain speaks up, "The Dark One says you're next."

That's my fucking girl.

CHAPTER 32
RAIN

urning around, I face the remaining petrified followers of The Chapel.

All cowards—the whole lot of them.

Pointing to the four immediately in front of me, "Pick him up and hold him down on the table like you have done with all of us in the past."

My tone surprises me, it's authoritative and confident. I want to smile with pride, but I resist. This isn't the time for celebration. People have been and are dying here tonight.

The selected four don't move.

They start elbowing each other, communicating as if to say *you go first*. It's evident now why they are here as followers, none of them could be leaders.

"Did she stutter? Leading up to tonight, you all called her *'your'* Principessa Oscura, when did that change?" Elijah's strong voice dominates the room while calling them out on their shit.

None of them respond.

Elijah picks his bat up, steps towards the four and his tone turns eerie. "That's what I thought. Now get the fuck over there and get this sack of shit on the table and keep him there."

"You ungrateful children," my father moans while still on the ground. The four I select scurry over and grab him by his arms and legs. He tries to fight it but is still groggy from being knocked out, his efforts are weak.

Elijah braces himself on the other side of the table as they lay my father's body down.

"You can't do this to me. I am your Master, release me at once, peasants!"

I clear my throat, "How does it feel? Being helpless, vulnerable and completely at my mercy?"

His head snaps towards me, spitting his words, "You are no child of mine."

"Sadly and regretfully, I am. But I wish I wasn't."

Elijah pounds both of his fists on top of the table. It shakes from his force. Looking at him, his head moves up slowly, his eyes glare and his face is hard.

"You are all as fucked as he is if any of you try to help him." He allows his words to sink in before continuing, "As for you Maxton, you delusional, egotistical, power-hungry con artist, by now I suspect you have guessed that I didn't bring Rain here because of The Dark One, or you really summoned her."

Elijah lowers his voice to a loud whisper and looks directly into my father's eyes, "Between the two of us, I think she's going to kill you."

A tiny laugh escapes me, I have not seen this side of E during kills before, and the sarcastic humor is an unexpected but pleasant surprise.

"He's right. I am. Perhaps I will have remorse after it's done, although I cannot be sure, yet. But The Dark One told us your name next, who are we to deny him, right father?"

Elijah bangs on the table again, this time more rapidly with his closed fists. Hysterical laughter erupts from his mouth.

My father's eyes widened in fear.

The four holding him down startle, and the pounding scares them further. The unpredictability of the situation adds to it. I fucking love it.

It's about time they all felt how it feels to be on the other side.

As Elijah stops pounding, the room goes completely silent, waiting to see what will come next.

Gripping the blade, I put the tip on the table and begin walking, circling it. The tip scrapes alongside me, only lifting it when passing one of the four holding him down. My eyes take him in, still draped in his black robe with the gold embellishment on the breast. Black dress shoes cover his feet.

As I reach Elijah, I whisper to him while keeping my eyes on my father, "Tear it open."

Leaning forward, E grips the middle of the robe on either side of the seam and rips it open. The buttons pop off and fly away. Throwing it open underneath, he is wearing matching black trousers and a shirt.

"Thank you." I whisper to E while touching his arm, signaling for him to step back again, that I've got this.

"Your mother would be ashamed, embarrassed even. Turning on your family like this?" My father taunts.

It works.

I react.

Before I can even think, I am slamming my blade into his armpit, which is directly in my line of vision thanks to the people holding his arms up.

A loud howl of pain follows.

Pulling the blade out, blood begins to soak into his shirt.

Instead of scolding him for speaking ill of my mother, the strong female who raised me, nurtured me and loved me until her last breath, I continue around the table until I reach the foot of it. His legs are spread, just like mine were that day before Elijah saved me.

It's time to show him how it feels.

Dragging my blade, I start just above his ankle on the inside of his leg. I apply enough pressure as I move it slowly up his leg to cut the fabric of his pants, which also leaves a shallow cut on his skin. It barely produces any blood.

Watching my movements, I am captivated. Going past his knee and up his thigh, I stop as I reach the pelvis area. Hovering the blade over his manhood, I outline a figure-eight pattern over it, skimming the thin fabric.

His hips try to shimmy to get me to stop and his breathing becomes louder. I can hear his brain racing, trying to think of what to say in order to make this stop.

Nothing will work.

His efforts would be futile.

Applying some pressure, his hips buck, "Please don't."

Slowly look up, my eyes move across his chest and reach his face, "Would you have stopped if I asked?"

Keeping eye contact, he doesn't respond. Which speaks louder than words and it is exactly what I expected.

Continuing on, I push the blade into his other leg, this time harder, and he winces. The tip cuts through the fabric and this time as I move down, blood trickles alongside. I know there is a major artery in the thigh. I hope I have hit it, but I have my doubts as blood isn't pouring out like I feel it would if I had. Which is fine, as it gives me more time to play.

As I finish with this leg, the tip of my blade is stained crimson red, and satisfaction washes over me instead of the remorse I thought I would be feeling right now.

Stepping out from between the two people holding his legs, I move around to the other side of the table.

Do I end this quickly or prolong his anguish?

Reaching the top of his head, I notice his hair is damp from where Elijah hit him with the bat, it's blood. I smile with pride. He is getting exactly what he deserves.

Gripping the handle of my dagger with both hands, I lift it over my head, keeping my eyes on the spot where I want it to go. Taking a deep breath in, as I exhale my arms lower with all my force behind them. As it pierces through his chest and stabs into his beating heart, it appears effortless as I watch myself, my hands wrapped around the handle. Pulling the blade out, I don't waste time slamming it back in, one after another, repeatedly.

Hearing the slice of the blade into his skin each time is calming. I feel so fucking alive.

Blood splatters from each stab decorate my face and white dress. It doesn't stop me, I keep going back for more. Relief and satisfaction wash over me.

A light touch graces my shoulder, breaking me

from my spell. I immediately let go of the dagger, the handle is sticking out of his chest. Looking down, blood is coming from his nose and mouth. I completely blocked everything out after the first stab.

If he screamed, I didn't hear it.

If someone told me to stop or that this was enough, I have no idea.

"You did so good, little bat. I am so fucking proud of you." E whispers in my ear as his arm wraps around my chest, pulling me closer to him, my back against his chest.

He rests his chin on my shoulder. "I am going to thoroughly fuck you later, our neighbors will hear your screams as I pound into your pussy and make you choke on my cock. When I am inside of you, I will go so deep you will feel me ramming against your cervix and you'll bruise."

As E makes his promises, he grinds against me, his hard cock brushing against my ass.

Raising my hand, I rub his face which is still resting on my shoulder. "Promise?" I tease.

He chuckles, letting me go and stepping back. His fingers trace the back of my thigh below my dress hem. He whispers back, his breath caressing the back of my neck, "Abso-fucking-lutely."

Chills run up my spine in excitement, and my pussy is wet with desire as he continues to trace along my skin.

Although the moment is broken as fast as it started.

Loud whispers come from the room. Elijah breaks his contact with me, stepping towards them, "You're all lucky you are in masks right now. If I knew who else was in the room while she was being cleansed, being fucking touched by him and then held down so his friends could get a taste, you would be joining him."

He looks back at me, smiling as he continues to speak, his tone is chilling, "You are all as fucked as he is if I ever find out who they were." Turning his head, he faces the crowd again, "If anyone is friends with the devil, it's me."

CHAPTER 33
ELIJAH

The need and desire to slaughter everyone else remaining is strong.

But I know I can't.

The police finding an absolute bloodbath of a scene would only send them in one direction, mine. Oh, what I would do to get away with something like that. Rubbing my face with my hand, I do what has to be done and not what I want done.

"I may not know who was here that day with Rain. But I do know who you all are. Where you live and what you love the most. I can find you and take that all away, fucking remember that when you leave here tonight still alive. One fuck up and you are gone. Your family, gone. Do you fucking understand me?"

In unison, they respond. "Yes."

"Good. Now get the fuck out of here."

A couple move, but a lot are unable to sense if I am bluffing or not.

"I said, fucking go!" I shout.

Wasting no time, they stumble about as they go to leave the space. Some are left behind, including those who fainted earlier. No one bothers to gather them, fucking selfish savages.

Turning around, the four who were tasked with holding down this son of a bitch are still at their posts.

"Are you deaf or stupid? GO!"

Knowing none of them are deaf, I know it's just stupidity. They let go of Maxton and join the others rushing to leave.

Taking in what is left in front of me fills me with absolute joy. Some people get high off drugs, I get my high from hurting people, from killing.

Bodies, blood, and death.

The fire still flickers, and the horrible smell that came with it earlier is either gone or I've gotten used to it.

"I couldn't stop. Once I stabbed him, I had to keep going and going."

Shock is setting in on Rain. Her hands shake, and blood stains them as she looks at them in disbelief. She has helped me hurt people and added to their pain before death, but never been solely responsible for taking a life like this.

"Passion, anger and impulse took over. It was like

watching poetry in motion as you let those sides free. So don't even think about beating yourself up over it. I won't fucking let you. This is exactly how everything was meant to happen. Do you understand me?"

I can't let her spiral. I don't understand what she is going through right now, I never will, but I will try everything to make sure she doesn't stay in this headspace for too long.

Her eyes move to the ground as she absorbs what I just said. It's only the truth, it's all I know. I couldn't lie to her about this if I wanted to.

"What if I accidentally do something like that to you? My mind disappears and my body just takes over and I can't stop."

She's scared of herself, interesting.

Walking over to her, I grip her chin with my fingers and tilt her face up so her eyes are looking into mine. Before I can speak, she does, "Your eyes are so unique. The blue with the brown specks. My favorite set of eyes."

This girl, fuck. Only she could melt me like this. Turn me into putty in her hands.

"You are never going to hurt me. Even if I piss you off so much that you feel like you could, because I know that will happen. But I also know, you won't hurt me."

Her eyes are screaming, *are you sure?*

"I'm positive." Reassuring her.

Her fragile voice is hushed, "Okay. I believe you." I chuckle, "You fucking better."

A beautiful smile forms on her face, it almost reaches her eyes. Considering the current situation, I can appreciate that she is trying.

Her eyes actually look inquisitive, what is my little bat thinking?

Raising my brows, I encourage her to speak up.

"You never got to use your bat." Her lips pout, she sounds disappointed for me.

"He got some action, hitting your dad in the head. Don't worry, little bat, sometimes he needs to sit back and take the supporting role."

A thunderous boom makes its way through the cave, interrupting this cute as fuck moment my girl has created. Rubble and dust fall from the ceiling.

"The cars." Is all I have to say for her to catch on. I almost forgot about setting them on fire.

Letting go of her, I position myself at the front of the long table where Maxton's corpse remains, pulling Rain's blade out of his chest. Blood continues to drip off of it as I push it through the belt loops of my pants, I don't bother wiping it off. Rolling him with a couple big pushes, his lifeless body dropping to the ground, landing overtop to his number three.

Undoing my belt buckle, then the button of my jeans Rain walks over and stands in front of me. Bracing herself on the table, she pushes herself up, and her dress rides up exposing her white panties. Spreading her legs, she leans back slightly and waits.

"My good little bat wants to fuck in her dead daddy's blood?"

She eagerly nods in delight. The mood has completely shifted.

Reaching up, I caress the soft skin above the neckline of her dress. Her eyes are already hooded in lust.

Using my fingers, I slide both straps off her shoulder and down her arm, where I lay them resting. Focusing back on her chest, her nipples harden through the thin fabric and my cock springs to life, realizing she also isn't wearing a bra.

Moving slowly, I move my fingers under the fabric and begin to tease her hard nipples. Brushing my fingers over them, I circle the area slowly causing her breathing to hitch. Gripping one between my fingers, I squeeze it hard enough so it stings. A soft moan comes from her slightly parted lips, which she is biting with her teeth.

Pulling one of her breasts out, exposing her, causes goosebumps to form along her skin. Taking advantage of the sensitivity, I lean forward and hold her nipple between my teeth, pulling on it slightly. Another delicious sound comes from her encouraging me.

Closing my lips around it, I lap it with my tongue, toying and teasing her. Her nails scrape on the wood, which is music to my ears.

My eyes wander up her body, as I admire her new collar and my blood decorated perfectly on her, I take my one hand, wrap it around her throat, just above the leather and squeeze it as I continue to suck on her sensitive breast. Her pulse is moving rapidly, the harder I suck, the tighter I squeeze, the faster it goes. The power she has given me is to never be taken for granted. As much as I may be tempted to in the moment seeing her wearing my blood, my collar, I would never betray her trust.

Letting go of her, I pull back raking my hand through my hair which has fallen over my forehead. Her hand reaches for me as she looks down, missing my touch.

Undoing my zipper, I pull my jeans down and free my throbbing cock. Squeezing it, precum leaks from the tip.

Grabbing hold of her waist, I hoist her off the table, spin her around and push her back down so she is bent over with her ass in the air.

Her head is turned and her cheek is resting in the blood.

Reaching under her white dress, I find the hem of her panties and pull them down. Taking a bent knee, I continue to slowly remove them from her legs. Tapping each of her ankles, she lifts one foot at a time as I slide them off. Bringing them up to my nose, I inhale her scent—fucking mine. Once satisfied, I shove them in my front pocket. I am keeping these.

Before standing up, I grip both her cheeks from underneath, squeezing and pushing them up. What a fucking sight!

Rain stands on the tip of her toes, pushing her back side out further. My face moves forward, and my lips brush against the soft, delicate skin of her ass. Grazing her now with my teeth, I open my mouth and bite into her.

"Fuck," she hisses.

Sinking my teeth into her flesh as I squeeze her harder sends my body into a frenzy. Feeling the skin crack, I lick the area and taste the familiar copper, which I now crave from her. Sucking, I get as much as I can into my mouth before pushing myself back. Regardless of how much I take from her, it will never be enough.

Standing up, I slap the area which is now red, bleeding and marked by me.

Rain pants, looking back at me with blood slowly dripping off her chin, "I want it tattooed on me. Your bite mark."

Reaching next to her, I rub my hand in her father's warm blood which was left behind from when he was still laying here.

My lips whisper, "Mine."

Which is my way of saying, I'm tattooing it on you

tonight. No fucking way am I letting anyone else get that close to her.

Continuing to coat my hand in the warm, thick, dark red blood, I push Rain's face back down so her cheek is against the hardwood. Using my finger, I trace a S on her forehead over some of the broken doll cracks I had drawn on previously, with the blood for Sinclair.

Sticking her tongue out, I take that same finger and place it in her mouth. Her lips close around me as she sucks, licking my finger and tasting the blood of our enemy. This is the hottest shit I have ever seen or had happen.

Rain Sinclair is without a doubt my dark soulmate.

Pulling myself free, I rub my hand quickly once more in the warm blood. I need to be inside her.

Leaning back up, I rub my hard, thick cock with the blood, using it as lube. Once satisfied, I circle her asshole with my thumb. Rain is still face down on the table, perfect for the taking.

Shoving my thumb in, I stretch her out, getting her ready for me.

A low groan leaves my mouth as she clamps around me and the invasion.

Oh little bat, this is nothing, you just wait.

Pulling out, I grip my cock, lining it up with her and slowly start to push myself in. Rain whimpers at the intrusion, which only makes me harder.

Gripping her hips, I use them to control myself as I

ease into her. Her ass is squeezing tightly around my cock as I get further inside of her. My balls hug against me, I won't last long once we start moving. Looking down, I wish I had a camera to take a picture. This is so fucking hot seeing her ass eating my cock like this. Sliding the last bit in, I hold still a moment longer, giving her a little more time to adjust. This is the first time I have taken her like this.

"Are you ready?" I whisper.

Panting, she responds softly, "Yes."

Pulling out slightly, I thrust back into her. Rain's back arches slightly as her head remains on the table. At first, I thought I could take this slow, but it's impossible.

"You like when your brother fucks your ass, little bat? You're being such a good fucking girl for me."

One of her hands reaches down, moving under her. Moving my hand along her arm, I reach where her fingers have gone, they are playing with her clit.

Instead of moving them out of the way, I let them stay and join her. Both of us are chasing her pleasure. As I chase mine from behind.

Our movements quicken, and beads of sweat begin to form on my face as my hair flops back over my forehead.

Rain moans with need the faster we work her swollen clit. My breath quickens, my heart is racing and I can no longer control my movements. Thrusting rapidly inside of her, I can't take my eyes off the sight below me. Everything about this is fucking perfect.

Rain's legs begin to shake, and her mouth opens with soft whimpers escaping. We continue circling her clit, working her through her release.

"Come for me." My voice rasps.

Her free hand clenched into a fist, "Keep going."

Yeah, like I would ever fucking stop.

Pleasure begins to flow through my body. Tingling up from the tips of my toes up my legs and to my spine. Throwing my head back, my eyes close from the overwhelming sensation.

Ropes of come start to shoot out of my cock as I chase my own release. Rain's pussy is dripping from hers.

Working her harder, I can hear the slapping of skin as my pelvis bounces off her ass.

"My dirty slut, you are all fucking mine."

"Yours E, always fucking yours."

My movements get slower, bending over her I rest my head against her back as my heart races. She grips my finger that was playing with her clit and brings it up to her mouth, sucking her release off it.

"You're playing with fire, little bat." I taunt her as she continues to tease me.

Her mouth smirks as she continues to suck my finger. My thumb rubs the side of her face in praise for being so fucking good.

Once we both have caught our breath, I stand up off her and she lets go of my finger. Pulling out of her, my cock is covered in blood and come. Not cleaning it off, I tuck myself back in and do up my pants.

Rain props herself up on her elbows, looking back at me, her eyes take me in.

"Thank you for saving me."

As I pull her dress back over her exposed skin, with my thumb I rub around where I bit her. It has dried up blood around the red, swollen area.

Looking into her hazel eyes, "I will always save you."

CHAPTER 34
RAIN

I don't regret a moment.

This has only validated what I already knew.

This is where I am meant to be.

As E slides my dress over my bottom, I begin to stand up and take in the scene before me once more.

Dark red blood drips off me and side of the table. The Devil, known as my father, is lifeless on the ground and his pathetic servant is lying dead next to him.

"We should get going." I suggest.

If the cars on fire exploding didn't alert anyone, the people who just left here have. I know E is untouchable, which I assume transfers over to me. But I would still rather not be caught at the scene of the crime.

Reaching down, Elijah grabs his bat. Walking

around the table, he bends again, this time coming back up with his hammer which is placed back under his belt to hang.

It has tiny pieces of skull fragments hanging off it. I prepare for it to turn my stomach as I stare, but it doesn't. I'm stronger than I thought.

Holding my hand out, he reaches behind him then places the dagger in my hand, which I thread through my black ribbon belt.

We don't say a single word to one another, but we move as if we have had an entire conversion.

E walks over to one of the followers who is still passed out and kicks them a couple times, "Hey, fucker wake up. Shows over. Go home."

The person doesn't move, I think they are awake but too scared to show it. Can't say I blame them.

Looking at the fire—the infamous fire which held so much meaning and power over The Chapel, now it no longer does.

I fucking hate this place.

"Can you light the table on fire?"

Hearing his footsteps behind me as the gravel crunches beneath his combat boots, I am trying to gauge which direction he is going. The flicking of his lighter tells me he is at the table.

Turning around, I watch as E, standing tall and hot as fuck in his tight jeans, top and combat boots. His skin, which is beautifully decorated in ink, including his face—I think that's my favorite. His hair flops over his forehead, fuck this view can't get any better and he's all mine.

Standing a few feet back, a large flame shoots out of his flamethrower and attaches itself to the wood.

Moving it slowly from one side of the table to the other, he makes sure to encase it all with fire. The areas where fresh blood remains light quicker than the rest, the flames roar to life feeding on it.

As he keeps his focus, he also questions, "Should I burn them too?" His chin motions to my father and his third, who are dead on the ground just behind the table.

"No. Leave them to rot." They deserve to have maggots and worms feasting on their flesh. Along with whatever other bug or rodent that needs a meal.

Elijah goes over the table once more before turning his thrower off and draping it back over his shoulder.

The few who passed out earlier still haven't moved.

Screw it, we will just leave them here.

Reaching out my hand, E walks over to me and laces our fingers together. His bat is back in his hand as he twiddles and rotates it. Walking through the archway, a massive weight leaves me, the worry, anger and negative energy are gone. Left behind where it belongs.

Swinging our hands back and forth, I start skipping down the long, dimly lit passageway that leads to where we are parked. I can feel E side-eyeing me like I am nuts but I know he's also watching my tits bounce, so I don't say anything, but I do throw a wink at him.

A familiar archway appears next to me, which causes me to freeze in place. We passed it before and I was so focused on why we were here that I didn't even notice.

Pulling on his hand, I dragged him through it, "Rain, are you sure?" He questions with unease.

"I need to see it one last time."

Letting out a loud sigh, he is frustrated but knows better than to stop me.

The steel bars come into view. Getting closer to where I was held, the door is propped open as the unlocked padlock hangs from it.

Reaching my fingers out, I brush them over the cold steel. Looking inside the space, I can see myself inside, defeated, mourning and timid. My stepmother was ready to lead me to a life sentence of imprisonment, to be kept by her husband, my father.

Then Elijah came and saved me.

Our connection since that night at my bar, has only gotten stronger.

He doesn't rush me which I appreciate, he allows me to take my time saying goodbye to the space that forever changed my life. Elijah will never understand how he had a hand in this, understanding feelings isn't something he can do automatically, but he is trying and maybe one day he will see what I see.

A fucking great person who does love hard. He is loyal—a tad over the top but that's what makes him uniquely E. And he is a great fuck.

Moving my hand from the bars, I brush his vial of blood which is now home around my neck.

I'm done. I'm ready to close this chapter and start the next.

He can feel it.

Guiding us out of the space, we step through the archway back into the main passage. But we aren't alone anymore.

Someone comes rushing from the entrance towards us, still in their black robe and white mask, "You won't get away with this. The Dark One will come for you!" They shout at us.

Elijah mumbles under his breath, "Fucking annoying." Then unlaces his fingers from mine.

Gripping his bat with both hands, he waits until the person gets closer and shouts back at them, "Well, my Dark One showed me that you are a fucking cunt." Then he smashes his bat against the person's head.

The person falls over, laying either dead or unconscious on the ground.

Elijah positions himself over them, one leg on either side of him. He raises his bat over his head and thrusts it down, beating their head with the wooden bat in quick succession. E's face is neutral until his last swing, when a tiny smirk forms.

At the same time, blood begins to pour out from behind the mask, pooling around their head.

E steps back over towards me and reaches his arm out.

Neither of us care as we grab each other's hands again, step over them and continue walking out.

"See, he got some action tonight."

A giggle escapes me from utter shock, "Wait, did Elijah Sinclair just make a joke?"

He doesn't humor me back, so I continue to bug him.

"Elijah Sinclair has a sense of humor. Alert the masses. He knows how to joke!"

He huffs, "I am going to enjoy disciplining you later, aren't I?"

Shit.

CHAPTER 35
RAIN

Looking in the rearview mirror, the beautiful flickers of orange, red and yellows get further away. The two cars E set on fire exploded and now a couple others are burning. Blackwood fire department is nowhere to be seen, there is no doubt they see the smoke. And knowing where it is coming from, they probably think it's some cult shit going on.

"Should we call it in?"

"No."

My dagger is sitting on my lap, and my white dress is now stained red. I won't wash it, I will archive it in a garment bag, preserve it for when we have kids and show them how their mom and dad met. The thought of kids catches me off guard.

"One day, little bat."

I want to question how he knows what I'm

thinking but I don't need to. We are just that connected.

Mind. Body. Soul.

The rest of the car ride home is quiet.

My body is exhausted, I could fall asleep but won't. I need to see my mom first.

Pulling onto the road our house is on, isolated just outside of town, trees surround the property, giving us privacy from prying eyes and curious minds.

E reaches to click the gate opener when a thought crosses my mind.

"Does this make us serial killers?"

Resting his head against the headrest of his seat, he turns to face me, "I've been considered a serial killer for years already, based on the standard definition the police use of three or more over a period of time of a month or longer. You, my little bat, have just joined the club this evening with your dad. Because you helped me with the other two. Congratulations."

Fuck.

The gates open and we pull up the long driveway to the house.

Elijah turns the car off but neither of us move.

"Ask your other question."

He knows I have more on my mind.

My voice comes out small, unsure how he will like this next one, "Was it hard? Killing your mom or forcing her to kill herself like that?"

Killing my father was terrifying at first when I thought about it, but once I started, I couldn't stop. But he knew his mom his entire life, I knew my dad for all of a couple weeks. He was my father by genetics only. There was no relationship or emotional attachment other than hatred when I thought of him. For everything he put me and my mom through.

Looking at E, he drops his head, playing with his thumbs in his lap, "No. She did this to herself, it's exactly how she deserved to go."

Tilting his head ever so slightly, his eyes squinted as if he were in pain, "She helped him. She brought you to him to be cleansed, to be fucking violated like that. She could have left. But she stayed, turning her back on her fucking kid by helping him. Don't for a fucking minute feel bad for her. I don't."

Chills run through me at his words. Goosebumps prickle along my skin.

He's right. She chose my father, a delusional narcissist, over her own son.

She truly believed in all the bullshit.

He did the right thing. She was no longer worthy of being his mom.

"I won't, I don't, I mean." Reassuring him.

Placing my hand in his, on his lap, rubbing the soft skin on the back of his hand, I need to get this out. "Thank you."

Gripping my fingers, he looks at me confused, the

shadows from the lighting outside only show me part of his face, "I protect what's mine. You never need to thank me for that, Rain."

"And I protect what's mine."

My comment makes him chuckle, "Baby, I don't need to be protected. The people who end up on my radar do, but it's already too late for them once I know their name, so it's of no use. But thank you, for wanting to protect me. No one's ever said that to me before."

As strong as he is, there is also a broken boy hiding deep inside.

I won't pry, not tonight. But one day, I hope he opens up more to me about it.

ELIJAH

"Are you okay?"

I don't know what possessed me to ask that. It's never been something I've said before - but with her - I want to know. I need to or I have to figure out a way to make sure she is ok. Her hand still clasped in mine, I take her lead and rub the back of her hand with my own thumb. It had a calming, soothing effect on me so I hope it has the same on her.

Being in her presence always does something to me.

"Yeah, I think so. Can we go see my mom? I want

to talk to her about tonight." Rain's demeanor changes, her energy has gone from uncertain of how she should feel to content, somber perhaps, and now she seems like a little girl eager to tell her mom about her day.

"Let's get you changed first, it's too cold for you to go out in just that. How does that sound, little bat?"

Her hand leaves mine and it cups my face. Her body leans over the center console, leaning in towards me. Her eyes take me in just as her perfectly pouty lips press against mine. Closing my eyes, I grip the back of her head, pushing us closer together. This kiss isn't ravenous or rough, instead it is soft and delicate. Something so strange to me yet so fucking familiar, reassuring, home. My heart drops briefly to the bottom of my stomach, it's from the initial discomfort. I'm not used to this kindness when being intimate like this.

We have had soft, quick pecks in our short time together but it's still taking me time to adjust. I don't fight it. I give in.

This is the kind of thing I never knew I needed, but again, she has shocked me by showing me I do.

Breaking our kiss, Rain pulls back just slightly. Her lips are still hovering over mine, and her warm breath moves across my skin.

Her hand is still pressed gently against my skin, my hand still on the back of her head and our foreheads lean into each other. A tingle of electricity is immediately felt as our skin touches.

"Let's go inside, my sweet boy."

Inhaling her sweet scent of vanilla and coconut mixed with the smokey smell from the fire, I nod my head against hers. "Whatever you want, little bat."

ain comes out the backdoor dressed in a pair of my sweats, rolled up at the waist and a cropped black hoodie showing her midriff. With a pair of black hightops and her hair still up, face still painted and splattered with dried blood. She looks fucking hot. The patio lights shine, and the rose gold from her collar catches some of the glare and shines briefly.

She kept it on. All my blood rushes down to my cock at the sight, at the knowledge that she's still wearing it, wearing me.

Turning the flashlight on, I start to walk, leading the way towards the special corner in the yard where her mom is. I need to add a path and garden lights so she can go and visit whenever she wants.

Our feet crunch against the grass, crickets chirp and the air is crisp against the skin.

Tonight is cold—colder than normal.

Maybe it has something to do with this evening, maybe it's just fucking cold out. I'm not one to question shit like that.

Her mom's grave comes into sight, and I stop in place, allowing Rain to go ahead so she can have some privacy while talking with her mom.

Her arm brushes against mine, she looks back at me, "Come."

Nodding my head, "Yeah, okay."

She walks in front of me as we take the last few steps. I shine the light on the area, holding it still so Rain can see.

As Rain lowers to the ground, she sits on her bum, hissing briefly from the sting of my bite, then crosses her legs, her elbows rest on her knees as her chin lowers into her hands. Standing behind her, we stay like this for a few moments until she starts to speak.

A loud breath gets blown out, "Where to begin." Her voice is faint.

"E, they aren't going to come for us, right?"

"No, little bat, they won't. Now stop worrying. We are safe. I promise."

All I can do is reassure her. There is nothing to show because no one will be coming. They haven't before and they will not start now.

"I'm safe. Elijah, he's kept me safe. It's done. It's over. He is dead." She pauses, gathering her thoughts before continuing, "I know you will always worry about me, you're my mom. But you can worry less now. I am safe. He can never get me or hurt us again. You should know what I did though. You might already, if you were there. I did it. I killed him. I used the same blade that was used on you. I needed your strength with me, thank you so much for giving it to me. The scary thing though, mom, is I don't feel bad about it. I thought I would feel remorse over it. I don't. Not over him. Not over the others."

I step closer to Rain, resting my hand on her head and rubbing it gently. She didn't need her mom's strength, she is strong enough without it.

She leans into my touch, her tone changes as she dives into the next topic, which catches me by surprise.

"Mom. I think I'm in love. And I think, once I show him what love is, he will see that he loves me too. Elijah got me this beautiful collar, it's black leather with gold accents and in the middle, a piece of him, encased in the most stunning glass vial. Our initials are engraved into the leather, I am a Sinclair now, mom. He has claimed me. I'm not alone. I will never be alone again."

Closing my eyes, her words feel overwhelming.

She's right, I don't know what love should look or

feel like. This strong pull and need to be around her, to possess and worship her, to fucking destroy any other person who looks at her like she's their next meal, that's what I know.

Is that love? I don't know.

"Okay, mom. I am tired and desperately need a shower. I am covered in dirt and blood and I feel like I stink. I love you and I'll come see you again tomorrow."

Rain places one hand on the ground in front of her. Then stands up, facing me, "Let's go shower."

RAIN

Warm water hits my skin as I stand in the shower.

As I wash my hair and body off, blood circled the drain. I'm not sure how long I have been standing here, but I'm not ready to move yet. The shower has a built-in seat as well, but I need to stand directly under the spray. Let it encompass my body as the glass around me steams.

My eyes are closed when I hear the shower door open.

Cold air invades my warmth, but only for a moment, until the door closes again.

Elijah.

Strong hands knead my shoulders and his hard cock pokes my backside.

I relax into him.

My head rests against his chest, and his hands move down my shoulders, squeezing them before sliding them down my arms.

His teeth bite my exposed earlobe before he whispers, "I need your tight pussy bouncing on my cock, now."

Elijah's voice is demanding. My pussy tingles, needing to give him what he wants.

Releasing me, his presence is gone.

Turning around, I see him sitting on the bench, leaning back against the shower wall with his strong legs spread and his large, hard cock laying against his abdomen.

My eyes take him in, he is so fucking hot. His tattoos cover him, my eyes stop on his bat wings on his arm, and then I look down at mine.

Smiling.

We are free.

"Get on my fucking cock, little bat. Don't make me ask again." My pussy aches, dripping at his demand.

Stepping between his legs, I hitch one knee on either side of him, using his shoulders for balance as I move to position myself over his cock.

As I begin to lower myself, I grip his hard cock with one of my hands, positioning it right where I need it. Rubbing his tip around the lips of my pussy, I tease him, which he doesn't like. Elijah's hand reaches up, gripping my throat.

I took my collar off for the shower, it felt so bare before his hand filled that void.

Squeezing, he speaks through his teeth, his eyes are serious, "Does my fuck toy not want to listen? Slide my cock inside of your pussy, or I will bend you over my knee and color your ass red. Edge you until your legs start to shake, then stop. Only to force you to suck me off until I explode in your mouth, until tears are running down your fucking face and you are covered in my come. Do you understand?"

Nodding my head, I position his tip at my entrance and begin to slowly slide down his length.

"Good fucking girl." He praises.

As I slide further down, I release my grip on his cock.

Throwing my head back, my long hair brushes against his thighs and his hands cup my breasts. Once I can feel him fully inside of me, my pussy tightens around him, not wanting to let him go. Moving my hips, I begin working him. Elijah's lips wrap around my nipple, nipping and pulling at it with his teeth as he mumbles against them, "Don't stop riding my cock until your legs are shaking and come is dripping out of you, coating me. Don't stop until you are begging, screaming my name, because you can't take anymore. And only then will I consider stopping. Because you are mine. Mine to have, mine to use."

His words send me into a frenzy.

E lets go of my breasts as I work him harder, his cock-piercing rubs just the right spots inside of me. The feeling is intense as I bury my head into his neck and use the wall for support.

His strong hands grip my hips, making our movements harder and faster.

Loud moans leave my mouth as my pussy continues working his cock.

"You can take it." He encourages between his own panting.

My hands move to his arms, and my finger nails dig into his skin as I drag them down his biceps.

E grips my hips harder, and I hope it leaves his marks. Our skin is slapping against each other, it's only amplified by the warm water showering over us.

"You're so fucking beautiful like this, little bat."

Those words send tingles down my spine and to my pussy. Closing my eyes, they roll to the back of my head as my orgasm hits me.

Biting Elijah's neck and we continue fucking through it, he only whispers, "Harder." If I bite any harder, I will draw blood. This orgasm is intense and I coat his big cock.

My legs are shaking, and I'm unsure if I am able to hold myself up any longer.

His release follows.

I can feel the ropes of his warm come coating my walls. His hands move from my hips to wrap his arms around my back, hugging our bodies closer together. We couldn't get any closer if we tried.

"Fuck, keep going. Never fucking stop." I whimper, letting go of my grip on his neck with my teeth. Another orgasm washes over me. My pussy continues to suck him in like a vacuum, never wanting to let go.

"Use me, little bat, fucking use me like I'm using you."

I do. Riding him through my release. I can feel our come mixing inside of me, I feel so fucking full.

His movements slow. As do mine, but my body is still shaking. He still has me wrapped tightly in his arms as his hips buck into me a couple more times before stopping.

I can feel his heart racing against me, it matches the pace of mine. This has to be the best sex I have ever had. This man knows my body better than I do.

Slowly, I bring my head up, opening my eyes as I take him in.

His eyes are closed, and as I brush his wet hair out of his face, he starts to open them. His face is red from the heat and the intense sex we just had. I'm sure mine's the same.

"Get off my cock and dry off. I still need to tattoo

my mark on your ass. Everyone needs to know who you fucking belong to."

Playfully, I slap his hard chest, "Ever the romantic Elijah Sinclair." Then kiss him on the cheek. As I rise off him, the feeling of his cock inside of me disappears. I miss it.

Our come drips out of me and as he becomes free, it hangs between his spread legs. He grips my head, pulling me to him and our lips crash. His tongue brushes against my lips and I let him in.

Devouring one another, we become each other's oxygen. Unable to get enough, we continue the passionate assault on each other's mouths. Moaning into his, he moans back into mine. Butterflies flicker inside of me, it sends that familiar tingle down my spine.

I pull back before we get lost in each other again. Because it will fucking happen. And I want that tattoo.

Winking before leaving the shower, he reaches out, slapping my ass which causes me to slightly jump from the sting. Stepping out, I turn back around quickly. Poking my head back in, "What are you waiting for? I need my marking, sweet boy."

He flips me off before laughing.

I fucking love this man.

Lying naked on our bed, the soft sheets under me feel wonderful against my skin.

The buzzing of the machine is soothing as Elijah tattoos his bite mark on me in red ink. The ass hurts more than I thought, but it's a quick tattoo so I will suck it up.

Scrolling on my phone, I get an idea.

"E, have you heard of a choke pear?" I ask casually.

The machine still buzzes but he stops tattooing, "Uh, yeah why?"

He sounds concerned.

"We should get one, for next time we bring someone back. Don't you think? Unless you already have one."

He doesn't respond.

"Actually, a lot of these ancient torture devices would be incredible to have. We should definitely look into others too."

I turn my head to look back at him. He is smiling, his sharp canines are even showing as he responds, radiating with pride.

"That's my fucking girl."

Rain is laying on our couch.

It's late into the night and my face is buried deep in her pussy. Her come is dripping down my chin as I am working her towards her third orgasm of the night. If I were to suffocate here and die, I wouldn't have picked a better way to go.

Her fingers are tangled in my thick hair, she grips it at the root as she continues to use my face, grinding rapidly against it as I suck her clit. One of my hands is squeezing her breast as hard as she is pulling on my hair. The other is under her leg which is propped up, and trembling rapidly next to me.

"Fuck yes. There. Don't fucking move from that spot," she pants while shouting at me.

Her release coats my face. I am a sticky fucking mess and love it.

As I stop sucking her clit, I start lapping her with my tongue, devouring her pussy until the very last drop comes out.

Her grip loosens on me as her leg falls to the side.

I look up at her, smiling.

She has no idea how badly I want to get her clit pierced. Maybe I'll do it one night when she's sleeping?

Her head is heavy on the pillow, with beads of sweat dancing on her face. Rain's chest moves rapidly as she continues to pant.

Whispering through closed lips, "No more. I can't take anymore."

Chuckling at her, I kiss her pussy before getting up. I don't wipe my face, this is too good to get rid of.

As I sit up on the couch, I grab a blanket, drape it over her and bring her legs to rest on top of my lap.

We sit in silence and I actually think she has passed out. Her eyes are still closed and her breathing has calmed. Watching her, I am interrupted by my phone. Grabbing it out of my pocket, I see it's my dad.

"Fuck."

If I don't answer, he will keep calling. And a part of me knows exactly why he's calling now.

"Yeah?" My tone is short. Not because I don't like him. Because I don't like what he is going to say.

That familiar deep voice responds, "It's time to come home, Elijah."

Rolling my eyes, I brush my hand over my face, "Can you get Rogers to make sure everything is ready and stocked?"

"He is already on it. Your place will be ready for the both of you."

Then he hangs up.

He knows I have been dreading this, no need to prolong the conversation on it.

Looking over to Rain, she looks peaceful and absolutely beautiful.

Tossing my phone next to me, I whisper to her, "If you thought your dad was fucked. Wait until you meet mine, you haven't seen shit yet."

The End.

Welcome to The Devil's Society.

Acknowledgments

And another one!
I've always wanted to say that - haha.
The show I watched on repeat while being inside
Elijah's mind was... An Idiot Abroad. It is a hilarious
British reality show. Easily 10+ years old, but I still
love it.

Welcome to my erotic horror era!
Thank YOU for reading Haunted by the Devil; The
Devil's Society.
Yes, more E is coming.
I am having the most fun right now. Elijah. Just typing
his name makes me smile. And Rain is the perfect
balance for him. The amount of tattoo's I already have
based on this book is also insane. But I love it.

Thank you to my fantastic team. I am incredibly
honored and appreciative of all your support each and
every single day.
From my ARC and Street Team, to my Alpha and Betas
and my handler the Bookland Goddess, Lori! And to
YOU the reader! Words will never be enough to
express my gratitude. So, for now, I hope thank you is
enough.

Special thanks to my Gypsy Beks and her handler
Daisie. Between us and Lori, the week leading up to
ARCs was filled with many sleepless nights and a lot of

energy drinks. Thank you ladies, for your sacrifices in order to get us here, Elijah being released into the world.

Mr. Kincaid. It's ok. Do not be alarmed. I'm fine. Everything is fine.
After he read Lessons, he asked if I got some of the torture idea's while looking at him. I straight face responded with, Yes. Purely for my own enjoyment and his reaction.
The questions I will get after this one should be fun.

This one is short and sweet.
I love you all.
You are all Queens, never forget that!

xx
kins

ps.
yes, this release was planned to line up with taylor's new album. i am a proud swifty 🤍

ABOUT THE AUTHOR

Kinsley is a Canadian, Dark Romance Author who dabbles in Taboo, Forbidden and is currently in her Horror Era. When she isn't plotting her next twisted book or watching true crime docs with her cats, you can find her working for the man. Reading. Or drinking wine while causing chaos with friends, let's not limit ourselves now. Make sure you follow Kins on her socials and sign up for her newsletter to see what is coming next!

authorkinsleykincaid.com

More from the Author

FORBIDDEN

Let's Play - Freebie

Within the Shadows

Lessons from the Depraved

Haunted by the Devil; The Devil's Society

TABOO

Wrecked

Sutton Asylum

Dark Temptation: Part One

Ghost Dick; A Port Canyon Chronicle

Dark Temptation: Part Two

Sick Obsession - Coming 2024

Fuck Me, Daddy; A Port Canyon Chronicle - TBD

Taboo & Audio can be found via authors website